Dance: Cinderella Retold

DEMELZA CARLTON

A book in the Romance a Medieval Fairy Tale series

This is a work of fiction. Names, characters, businesses, places, events and incidents are either the products of the author's imagination or used in a fictitious manner. Any resemblance to actual persons, living or dead, or actual events is purely coincidental.

Copyright © 2017 Demelza Carlton

Lost Plot Press

All rights reserved.

ISBN-13: 978-1985289338

ISBN-10: 1985289334

DEDICATION

This book is dedicated to May.
No one else was crazy enough to encourage me to live
the fairy tale.

One

"Now your father must teach you to dance." The words rang like a bell in Mai's head, for they were the last thing her mother said to her before she died.

But her father showed no signs of teaching her anything, if in fact he noticed her at all. So deeply was he mired in his grief that Mai wondered if he even remembered he had a daughter. He moved from snake to dragon to tiger, each pose as graceful as the last, until Father became a fighter and nothing more. She knew his prowess in battle honoured the ancestors and that Mother was one of them now, but with each blow he aimed at the air, he dishonoured her last wishes.

Mai was only a little girl, but she had made promises to her mother, too. She had vowed to love, care for and honour her father. So her sense of duty made her step into the courtyard and face the furious man who fought ghosts. His hand stopped a breath from her face.

"You should not be here, child," he said, his voice raw and breathless.

Her dark eyes brimmed with hope. "I wish to dance, too, Father," she said. "Show me."

He shook his head. "I only know the martial dance. It is the dance for highborn sons, not daughters."

"Mother said you must teach me."

Father dropped to his knees. "If it was her wish, then I must."

In the mud of the courtyard, Mai found her father again. His instructions seemed strange at first, but as her movements became more practiced and fluid, she understood that this was a dance, if different to the dances her mother had excelled in.

Every morning, she joined her father in the courtyard for their daily dance until the sun rose above the house walls and set his grey hair aglow. Many moons passed in this way, until one summer dawn. Father smiled, then he laughed and said, "You have your mother's grace, Mai. If she had ever picked up a sword, she would have been both deadly and beautiful."

Mai felt his eyes on her, reading her soul.

"I will not always be able to protect you, so perhaps it is fitting that you learn all that I can teach you, before I join the ancestors and your mother."

"You are not…" She swallowed. "You're not ill, are you, Father?"

"No, I'm not. But we never know how much time we will have, so we must make the most of it." He bowed his head. "Today, I will go on a journey. The new Emperor summons me to court, and I must obey."

Mai swallowed hard, blinking back tears. "Yes, Father. I will pray to Mother every day until you return."

Father smiled down sadly at his young daughter. "Living or dead, she will always bring me home."

Two

Months passed, for it was a long journey from their mountain village to the capital. Every morning, Mai made an offering at the ancestral shrine, before moving to the courtyard to practice dancing alone. If she closed her eyes, she could almost believe her father practised beside her, and she longed for the day when he would return.

One evening, as she placed her mother's favourite flowers in the shrine, she heard a commotion in the distance. She followed the shouts to the gate, where she could see what looked like a procession making its way through the village. Her heart stuttered in fear. Surely…not a funeral procession?

None of the people headed toward her house was wearing white, she realised with relief, for even under the dust caking their clothes, the colours shone through.

Then something appeared around the corner of the last house in the village that made Mai stare even more intently. A box as big as a house, sitting on poles carried by several men, brought up the rear of the procession. This, too, was brightly coloured in red and gold, though dulled with the dust of travel. Curtains swayed in the doorway to the box, tempting Mai to climb inside.

The procession reached the gate and she raced across the courtyard to the veranda, where she would have a better view of everyone as they crowded into the yard. Especially the mysterious box.

The box bearers set their burden on the ground, right in front of the veranda steps. A man stepped forward and stuck his arm through the curtains, then pulled it out again, clasping a hand.

At the bottom of the curtains, a tiny, striped shoe poked out, not much larger than one of Mai's shoes. She clapped her hands in delight, hoping for a playmate. Yet the girl who emerged from the box was far older than Mai – she was a woman grown, despite her tiny feet. And the way her round belly bulged through her robes told Mai the girl would be a mother before long, just like the other women in the village. The woman swept past into the house without noticing Mai.

Mai sighed and sat down. No other children to play with, no mother to tell her stories, and no father to dance with. The servants wouldn't play with her, either. A more morose girl would have sat there and sulked, but Mai was a cheerful child, so instead she rose and made her way to the family shrine. Her mother might not be able to tell her stories, but she could tell her mother one, about the arrival of the round-bellied girl with the tiny feet.

Mai gathered some flowers from the garden and climbed the steps to the shrine, only to discover she wasn't the only one paying her respects to the ancestors.

"Father!" she exclaimed, racing across the tiles to throw herself into Fu's open arms. "I came to tell mother about the new girl!"

"Her name is Jing, and she will be your new stepmother," Fu said gravely.

Mai squirmed out of his grasp so she could stare up at him. "That girl is not my mother. She'll be mother to the babies in her round belly, just like Mrs Wu in the village."

"No, she is not your mother, and yes, she will give you sisters to play with. But Jing is used to life in the

Imperial City, not a country house like ours. Will you do your best to help her, like a good daughter?" Fu asked.

"For you, Father, anything. She is our guest, and we must be hospitable to guests," Mai declared.

Fu laughed softly. "No, child, she is not a guest. Jing is here to stay. This is her home now, but I think she would like it if you treated her like an honoured guest." He eyed her. "She does not rise early, for court women don't like to see the dawn. So we will resume our dancing lessons tomorrow at dawn. The army with the best trained troops is assured victory, remember. Have you practised while I've been gone?"

Mai nodded happily. "Every morning, Father. It is not as much fun by myself, but now you are back, it will be better."

"Do you use your wooden sword every morning?" Fu demanded, eyeing Mai's thin arms.

She shook her head. "No, for it is too heavy."

"It is at first, but as your strength increases, you will grow used to it. A dancer's skill is equal parts balance and strength. Your balance is good, but we must work on your strength."

Mai bowed her head. "Yes, Father. I will practise now, so that tomorrow morning I will be ready."

He clapped her on the shoulder. "Good girl." Fu glanced at her mother's funeral tablet. "Da Ying would be proud to see you dance."

Mai beamed. "Thank you!" She skipped out into the courtyard in search of her practice sword, forgetting about stepmothers or sisters or strange boxes, for they were nothing compared to the honour she intended to bring her ancestors.

Three

For the most part, Jing left Mai alone. Her increasingly rounded belly made her waddle around like the ducks in the pond at the bottom of the garden, to Mai's amusement, until one night Mai woke to shrill howls as first one, and then the other of her two half-sisters were born.

Lin and Lei's cries could be heard echoing through the house at all hours of the day and night, while Jing and the servants did everything in their power to quiet the babies.

Most days, Father could be found in the courtyard, training, as he had when Mai's mother had died, once again with a deep frown on his face. The frown turned into a smile whenever Mai joined him, though, and everything seemed right in the world once more.

For six years, they danced together every morning and night, as the two screaming babies turned into troublesome toddlers before growing into girls the same age as Mai had been when her stepmother first arrived. But when a child's piercing scream broke the dawn silence, Mai laid down her wooden practice sword and dashed into the house, certain Lin or Lei had been seriously hurt.

She found a manservant holding down Lei while Jing did something to the girl's feet that only made her howl louder. Jing shouted for bandages, which a maid handed to her. Jing wrapped the strips of silk around her daughter's feet before cramming them into a pair of shoes that even Mai knew were too small for her.

Lin watched with wide eyes until the manservant let go of her sister and seized her instead. Then Lin started to cry and struggle, begging her mother not to hurt her.

Jing grabbed the girl's shoulders. "Do you want to be a lady, and find a good husband, or be doomed to be an old maid like your sister Mai?"

"I don't need a husband," Mai protested. "I promised my mother I would take care of Father, always."

"There. Do you want to be a drudge all your life, or

a lady who is carried everywhere in a litter?" Jing pressed.

Lin stopped struggling. "I want to be a lady, and a bride to a handsome husband, just like in the stories," she whispered.

She climbed up beside the still-sobbing Lei and Mai watched in horror as Jing broke her daughter's toes, bent them beneath the soles of her feet and bound the whole mess up in silk bandages. Now Mai understood why the too-small shoes suddenly fit Lei again, for Lin's shoes slid on over the bandages as if she were years younger.

"There," Jing said, planting her hands on her hips. "Now, you must walk around the garden ten times before you may have breakfast. Go, go!" She shooed the girls off the bed.

Both of them cried out as they took their first steps, begging their mother to let them sit down again, for their feet hurt too much to walk.

"Ladies must have lotus feet like mine, or no husband will have you," Jing said. "You will walk, no matter how much it hurts, or you will not eat. Do you hear me?"

Both girls nodded. Holding hands, they hobbled outside.

Mai folded her arms across her chest. "How can you do such a thing to your own daughters? It is barbaric!"

When Jing turned to face her, Mai was surprised to see tears streaming down her stepmother's face. "I do what must be done, to give my girls a future. A little pain now is nothing compared to a lifetime of being unwanted. My mother spared me until my feet had almost grown too big, and I was lucky to get a husband at all. If not for the Emperor's command and your father's ignorance of court fashions, I would not have been married, for no other nobleman would have me. My daughters will have such tiny feet that even princes will marvel at them."

Mai drew herself up. "You will not do such a thing to me. If you try to touch my feet, I will make you rue the day you were born." She wasn't sure how, but she had heard a great hero in one of her father's stories say such a thing, so it must mean something very frightening.

Jing sagged, looking as haggard as though it was her own toes that had been broken today and not her daughters'. "No, I will not," she agreed. "You are too old, and your feet are too big. I should have bound your feet when I first came, but my pregnancy and the girls…I could not. You will never find a good husband now, Mai. Not with feet as big as yours. Just like your common-born mother."

"My mother was not common! She was a general's

daughter, like me, and her feet were perfectly sized to suit my father!" Mai snapped.

Jing marched to the cupboard and took down a pair of shoes Mai recognised as her mother's favourite. Beside them, Jing placed a pair of her own. "Times have changed since your mother was a girl. Perhaps she could make a good marriage with feet like this, but we have a new Emperor now, and in his court, they would call her an iron lotus, fit only to marry a fieldhand."

Mai stared at her mother's red silk shoes beside Jing's tiny striped slippers. "My mother's shoes were magical. She wore those the night my father fell in love with her, she said, and she kept them. She said the ancestors had blessed them with balance in all things, so that when she wore them, her balance was perfect, too."

Jing shook her head. "You don't understand, do you? It doesn't matter how well a girl dances any more. It is all about the size of her feet. You will never marry." She thrust the shoes at Mai. "Take these huge things away. Treasure them if you must, as a memory of times that will never come again. No amount of magic in your mother's shoes will make you marriageable. When you pray to the ancestors, pray that I bear your father a son, for with no husband, you will have no children to take care of you in your old age. No one to bring flowers to your shrine once you are gone."

Jing tossed her head and minced away before Mai could reply.

Weighted down with sorrow that her stepmother could hurt her sisters so, Mai made her way back to the courtyard. Her father was nowhere to be seen and her two sobbing sisters had collapsed on the steps, in too much pain to continue their tortuous circuit. She beckoned a maid over to tend to the girls, before resuming her search for her father. He would put a stop to this, she was certain.

Mai found her father in the shrine, lighting her mother's favourite incense. Normally, she waited until he was finished praying, but her sisters' pain would not wait. "Do you know what she has done?" Mai demanded. "She is torturing the girls. Breaking their bones! They will never learn to dance as you taught me. They can barely walk! And for what? To find husbands? What husband would ask for his wife to have her feet broken when she's just a baby, long before he even meets her, so she can wear smaller shoes?"

Father shook his head. "The new Emperor is nothing like the old. Many things have changed. Jing swears to me what she does is for our daughters' future. A future I fear I do not understand any more. I will not fight when I cannot win. The court of my youth is gone, along with the Emperor I served. It is a strange new world we live in, Mai. Your mother and I sought to protect you from it, but…" He squinted at her. "Are those her shoes?"

With trembling hands, Mai surrendered the shoes to her father. "Is it true that she wore them the night you fell in love?"

"She wore these every night, and every day, too," Father said. "I never saw her in any others until we were married. They were a gift from her fairy godmother, she said, enchanted with balance. Her godmother gave them to her after she got in trouble for losing her shoes. These shoes can never be lost. They will always find their way back to their rightful owner." He glanced down. "They should fit you now. Why don't you try them on?"

Wear her mother's magical shoes? Mai's breath caught in her throat, but she did as her father told her. Slipping one bare foot, then the other into the shoes, she found he was right. They fit her perfectly.

"You will be as beautiful as your mother one day, and even more graceful, I think. When it is time to find a husband for you, I will have plenty of men to choose from, who would beg for your hand," Father said.

"I don't want a husband, Father. I promised

Mother I would take care of you," Mai replied mutinously, pressing her lips together.

"That is Jing's job now," Father said with a sigh. "And her son, if she manages to bear one. You are young yet. A man might catch your eye the way I caught your mother's eye. Then, I will have no choice but to make the match you choose."

Mai looked her father in the eye. "I will never choose another man over you, Father. I promise."

Fu kissed the top of his daughter's head. "You are a good girl. Do not think too harshly of your stepmother. Your mother wanted you prepared for a different life, while your sisters will find husbands at court, like their mother did. Court life requires sacrifices that I hope you will never have to make."

He had that right, Mai thought but did not say. Not if all her ancestors and every dragon in the country teamed up to drag her to the Emperor's palace would she set foot inside the place. Especially if she had to bind bits of her body and pretend to be something she wasn't.

Four

Years passed as Jing taught her daughters court dances for their absurdly tiny feet, and Mai practised increasingly complex martial dances with her father. On her sixteenth birthday, he gave her a sword made especially for her. While Mai stood speechless with joy at such a thoughtful gift, her stepmother trotted into the courtyard with a scowl on her face.

"That is not a suitable gift for a girl!" Jing said. Ten years had not been kind to her. She had tried to give Fu more children, but none of them survived very long. "You should return it to the armoury, to await the birth of your son." She patted her belly with considerable satisfaction.

Mai suppressed a groan. When Jing was pregnant, she made Mai do everything for her, including running errands she should send servants to do. Though she knew her father wanted a son, she hoped Jing would miscarry early this time, instead of giving birth to a stillborn child. Better than nine months of hope only to have them dashed at the end.

"If you bear me a son, my blacksmith will craft him his own sword," Fu said firmly. "This belongs to Mai. She needs it to practice, for a wooden sword is no longer enough."

"She needs a husband," Jing grumbled, shuffling back inside.

"For your next birthday, I will see about finding you a husband," Father said. "But in the meantime…will you dance with me, Mai?"

Mai smiled. "Gladly, Father."

Five

Jing's time came early and the house rang with her screams even as the midwife tried to quiet her. Mai's father prayed in the shrine, where he could not hear the screaming, so when a messenger arrived at the gate, it was up to Mai to meet the man.

He wore the Emperor's colours of red and gold, and the scroll case he carried on his belt blended in with his robes so completely Mai almost didn't see it until he reached for it.

She instinctively dropped into a defensive pose, thinking that he was reaching for a blade.

The man laughed. "Easy, boy. I bring a message from the Emperor. Though it is a declaration of war, it is not war on Yeong Fu, but a call for him to provide troops. Perhaps if you are lucky, he will send you."

Mai opened her mouth to tell the messenger that she was no boy, nor would her father waste her life in a war against the rebellious cities to the north, but a particularly loud scream issued from the house.

"Sounds like war is already here," the messenger commented. He thrust a scroll into her hands. "Your father might go to war just to get some peace and quiet." Laughing to himself, the man headed down the road toward the town.

Mai itched to unfasten the scroll and read the message it contained, but not even she dared to break the Emperor's seal. Instead, she carried it to her father where he knelt in the family shrine.

"What is it? Another dead daughter?" Fu asked without turning around.

Mai moistened her dry mouth. "No, Father. It is a summons from the Emperor. Calling you to war."

Fu made a disgusted sound. "No doubt throwing more lives away, trying to reclaim one of the lost cities in the north when it is too little, too late. Only a strategist like your mother could take those northern cities, but not even she could devise a way to hold them. The northerners breed so much faster than we do, and their would-be king sends them against us in greater and greater numbers. Better to broker a treaty than to besiege some northern city. The worst policy is to attack cities, as any decent general should know."

"But he is calling you to war, Father. You are the greatest general in the kingdom." Mai dropped to her knees beside her father. "If anyone can win, it is you." Mai's eyes shone with admiration as she gazed at him.

"The man who now calls himself Emperor made me retire when he foisted Jing on me. He ordered me to go home and sire sons to serve him as I served his father." Fu waved angrily in the direction of the house. "Even my stillborn sons are too smart to die in that man's service. They would rather founder in their mother's womb, and I cannot blame them. Let him take my sons, for the Emperor will not have me for this stupidity!"

A breathless maid entered the shrine, bowing deeply. "Master, young mistress. The mistress has given birth to a son!"

A live one, Mai presumed, by light of the Jia's joyful expression.

"Come, I must see this for myself," Fu said, rising. He led the way into the house, with Mai and the maid following close behind.

Jing lay in bed, a gloating smile on her face as she regarded the tiny, wrinkled baby in her arms, oblivious to the army of maids carrying out bloodied sheets and replacing the soiled linen around her.

"I have given you a son, husband," Jing said, pride dripping from her every word. She held the squirming child out for his inspection. "I have named him Yeong Fu, after his father."

Fu laughed mirthlessly. "And when the Emperor sends more troops to take Yeong Fu to war, I will offer him my son. For this baby here will grow to manhood before General Li retakes the city he lost."

Jing's eyes grew wide as she swaddled the baby tightly. "What is this?"

"The Emperor has summoned me to recruit and lead an army of reinforcements north to assist General Li's siege of Dean," Fu said.

Jing clapped a hand to her mouth. "So you are going to war? How soon?"

Fu laughed. "I am not going anywhere, woman. Did I not say I would offer the Emperor my infant son in my stead? If he'd sent the Empress herself to command the siege, it might have a better chance than the one led by her brother."

Mai stared in wonder as Jing's eyes widened further. "But you cannot disobey the Emperor!" Jing cried.

"I can, and I have. He thinks he can send me to certain death under that fool's command. If the army doesn't die of disease or starvation, the garrison of Dean will cut them down just as they did last time. The Emperor sends me so that he may blame someone else for General Li's mistakes. It will not be me!" Fu's voice rose to a roar and baby Fu began to cry. Father strode out of the room, swearing under his breath about fools and those who didn't understand the first thing about war.

Mai turned to follow him out.

"You have to convince him to change his mind," Jing said. "Mai, you must. Or we all will die."

Mai stopped, and shot a scornful glance at her stepmother. "You don't understand the first thing about war. If Father says this is foolish, then it is."

"More foolish to disobey the Emperor than to go to war," Jing insisted. "In battle, men live or die, but when the Emperor sends his troops to crush a defenceless household like this one, not a fortified city, we will be slaughtered. You may play with swords in the yard, but one girl cannot hold off an army."

For once, Jing was right. Mai could best her father in training, but not an army of highly trained troops. And she didn't want to die. "I will ask him," she said.

Six

She didn't need to look far for her father, for Fu had chosen to take out his frustrations in a furious training session in the courtyard. Mai took up her sword and joined him, shifting from pose to pose as effortlessly as her father.

"You are a better fighter than me now," Fu said grudgingly.

Mai bowed her head at the compliment. "Thank you, Father, but I still have a lot to learn. I hope to live long enough to do so, though. Jing says that if you disobey the Emperor, he will send an army to kill us all. Even you and I together are no match for an army." She glanced around the yard. "And there is nowhere we can retreat to from their superior numbers here."

Fu lowered his blade. "Jing sees only a small part of the picture. Your mother would see it all, and know how to act, but without her, I have no grand strategy any more." He sighed. "If I disobey, one day the Emperor may send an army, if he is not too busy making war on cities where he has no business being. But if I obey him, my dishonour is certain. General Li is the Empress' brother and for all that he is a fool, he still commands the respect of his army. If I were to arrive at the siege of Dean, I would be under his command. When he offers battle, he will lose, just like he did the first time he besieged the city. And he will lay the blame on me. Perhaps my inexperienced troops, or my poor commands, or my insubordination, for I will not take orders from a fool. When word reaches the Emperor, he will move swiftly to seize my lands and all who live on them. He will kill my family, and he will kill me, because he only holds power as long as General Li is his ally. If I ride to war, we will all most certainly die. And if I do not...we at least stand a chance that the Emperor will forget about us. For the best chance of victory, a general must know when to attack, and when to defend, and when not to fight at all." He bowed his head. "Mai, this is not the time for fighting."

"A general who fears defeat cannot be victorious," Mai replied. "That is what you taught me, Father. The hope of victory will only result in defeat. It is strategy and planning that win, every time. And hoping to be forgotten…is no plan at all."

Fu smiled sadly and shook his head. "For a moment, I saw your mother looking out through your eyes. She always had a clear view to victory. Always. But without her…I am lost. If you were my son, I would send you in my place, so that you could learn the truth of war on a battlefield instead of just a training ground. True victory must be won, and contrary to what General Li believes, the best victories are bloodless ones."

Mai shook her head. "How can you win a victory without spilling any blood?"

"Through winning the hearts of your enemies," Fu replied. "I should send you to court as my messenger. Perhaps you could win the heart of the Emperor, or one of his sons. Maybe there is hope after all. I shall think on it, and tomorrow we will make plans to send you to court. For now, go see your stepmother, and tell her what I have told you." He shooed her away.

Mai's head spun. Sending her to court to seduce the Emperor? What hope did she have? Jing commented on her unmarriageable feet every time she saw her, until Mai knew no man would look on her as a possible wife, let alone a prince or the Emperor. She was better suited to war, like her mother.

If only she was a boy and not a girl…

"What did he say? Did you change his mind?" Jing demanded when Mai returned to her stepmother's room.

Mai shook her head. "He will not go to war. He wants to send me to court to be the Emperor's concubine instead, I think." She felt sick at the thought.

Jing snorted. "You? The Emperor would not even look at you. No man wants a wife or a concubine who plays with swords."

"There was one who did," Mai said slowly. "Long ago, when Sunxi first wrote his treatise on war, the Emperor asked him to prove it by training his concubines in the art of war. And he did."

Jing waved the words away like a bad smell. "That is nothing but a story. Soldiers carry swords, concubines need to be pretty. Your sisters will have all the accomplishments and beauty a girl needs to charm a prince, when they are old enough, but not you. You would do better to take up a sword and lead an army in your father's place. In court, you will only make enemies. More than we have already."

For a moment, Mai's heart soared at the thought of commanding an army, as her father had done. As her mother had, too, or so she'd said. When her father had fallen in battle with a near-mortal wound, she had rallied his troops to victory. Mai had studied ever tenet in Sunxi's treatise and trained every day for more than a decade. Why couldn't she command troops in her father's stead?

Because no army would follow a woman, not even the daughter of Yeong Fu and Da Ying. If she were truly a boy like the messenger had first assumed…

Mai raised her head and met her stepmother's gaze. "I will. I will dress in men's clothing and take up my sword and take Father's place. It is the only way."

As the words left her lips, Mai knew they were the right ones. She could bring no honour on her family here. But if she was victorious in battle…or even died bravely in battle, she would honour her ancestors and her mother by her deeds.

Jing's mouth fell open in shock. "You are too small to pass for a man. And your breasts…" Mai expected her stepmother to launch into a scathing lecture about the size of Mai's breasts, whose only virtue, according to Jing, was that they made Mai's feet seem small, but the lecture never came. "You must bind them, but an illusion would be better." Jing bit her lip. "Yes, I think I can do it."

"An illusion? What do you mean?"

Jing smiled, revealing blood on her teeth that had

not been there before. "I shall cast an illusion, so that all who see you or your clothing while it is near you will believe you to be a man."

"But…surely only a witch could do something like that…" Mai faltered. She swallowed. "Are you a witch? Can you make me into a man?"

Jing made an impatient sound. "I cannot turn you into a man, girl. I am a witch, not a powerful enchantress, and a weak one at that. I can make things look like they do not, but I cannot change you. Do you want to look like a man, join the army and save your family?"

Mai lifted her chin. "I do. All warfare is based on deception."

Jing rolled her eyes. "You should have been born a boy. I can make you look like one, but you will have to make them believe you are a man, and not a girl. If the soldiers find out you are a girl, you will become nothing but a common whore. If they don't kill you." She wet her lips. "Either way, you will dishonour your family, so you will not be welcome back here."

Mai nodded. "I understand." And she did. She would not dishonour her mother or her ancestors. Da Ying's and Yeong Fu's daughter could only be victorious. It was in her blood.

Seven

Mai flexed her arms as she donned her mother's armour, amazed at the play of muscles she'd never seen on her arms before. No matter how much Jing said it was an illusion, they looked and even felt real. She itched to try lifting something heavy, like one of the big urns in the garden. It probably helped that she'd bound her breasts flat under her shirt, too. She felt…manly.

Even her mother's shoes had taken a more masculine appearance. They looked more like something her father would wear than the pretty silk slippers she knew and loved. Yet if she closed her eyes, she felt exactly the same. Her balance was the same as ever, and that was what mattered. She buckled on her sword belt and drew the blade from its sheath.

"Be swift as the wind. Plunder like fire, stand as firm as the mountains, and move like a thunderbolt," she whispered, as she did at the beginning of every dance.

She moved through the sequence of morning exercises she'd performed every day for as long as she could remember, noting the places where her armour restricted her movement, few though they were.

In the stable, she found her father's warhorse, saddled, packed and ready, as Jing had promised. Staring up at the huge animal, Mai almost doubled over as doubt punched her in the belly. She shouldn't be doing this. Girls didn't ride to war. If anyone in the army found out, she was as good as dead – to her family, even if she still breathed. It was one thing to spar with her father, who surely had gone easy on his daughter, but to fight armed soldiers in battle? She would die in a heartbeat. Now Mai felt queasy, too. If she rode to war, she would never return. Never see her family again. Her stepmother. Her sisters. Her father…

Mai wanted to run to the shrine, where she knew she would find her father, to bid goodbye to him one last time.

But she could not. If her father saw her like this, he

would stop her. Even if it killed her, she had a duty to save her family from the Emperor's wrath.

She found the messenger camped just outside of town, on the outskirts of what looked like an army camp in a fallow field. Some of the men she recognised from the village, but most of them were unfamiliar. There were more men in this one field than in the entire village where she'd grown up. More than enough to slaughter her father's household, if commanded to do so.

All she had to do was walk in, and convince the men she was one of them.

Her heart sank, but Mai took a deep breath as she dredged up her courage. "All war is deception," she reminded herself under her breath. She rode up to the messenger's tent, reined in her horse and managed to dismount without falling. "My father sent me to captain his troops," she announced.

The messenger laughed. "And how many wars have you served in, boy?"

Mai felt her face redden. She hoped Jing's illusion hid that. "None," she admitted. "But my father has been training me for battle since I was six."

"Did you learn much?"

"Some," she said. "He said I could train for a lifetime, but learn more on one battlefield than in a decade of practice." She lifted her chin. "That is why he sent me."

This seemed to satisfy the messenger. "What's your name, boy?"

"Yeong Ma…oh!" Mai clapped a hand over her mouth in horror. She hadn't been here a minute and already she was about to reveal her identity.

"Yeong Mao?"

"Yyyes?"

"That is your name?" the messenger asked.

Mai nodded, not trusting her voice.

"I hope baldness doesn't run in your family, then. It would be a great pity to have a name meaning thick hair when you have none. Your men would have no respect for a general with a funny name." The messenger laughed, then gestured at the grass behind his tent. "You may set up camp beside me. In the morning, we march for Dean."

"Don't I get to decide when my men move?" Mai asked.

The messenger laughed so hard, he almost bent double. "These are not your men any more, boy. They belong to General Li, as do you. When we reach his camp, he'll make the decisions. My orders are to bring reinforcements, and I will. Untrained farm boys, most of them, but once the general's captains are done training them, even you might manage to kill a man in battle. Or die trying."

Mai smiled wanly and tried to hold back her tears as she led her horse to what would be her campsite for the night. Men did not cry, she told herself. At least, not where anyone could see. Once she had her tent set up, then she could go to pieces at the thought of killing people. That she might die, she had come to accept, but that other men must die at her hands? The very thought made her shudder.

But if a stranger had to die to protect her family…so be it, Mai decided. There was nothing she would not do for those she loved. She might be a girl, but when the time came, she would have the heart of a warrior, until her heart beat its last.

Eight

"There is no greater pleasure than thrusting your sword hilt-deep in another man's heart," Prince Yi declared, demonstrating.

"My advisers told me you had never been with a woman before, but now I begin to believe it," Emperor Yun replied. "No wonder you don't have any sons yet. You're supposed to do the thrusting lower down, and into a woman."

"I don't slaughter women. I fight enemy soldiers in battle, and bring honour to our family name when I am victorious. That is my purpose, Father," Yi said, yanking his sword free of the practice dummy. A shower of straw came with it.

The Emperor sighed. "I know that is what you have done, but I have more than enough generals. What I do not have is a suitably married heir to the throne, with children of his own to ensure the succession of our dynasty."

Yi's hands clenched around his sword. He whirled and lopped off the practice dummy's head. He wanted to hack the hapless straw man to pieces, but he feared even that would not soothe his frustration. "And what if I don't want to marry anyone, Father, let alone some suitable girl? Every maiden in court has feet so tiny she trots like a pig on its hind legs, and all they seem able to do is dance and giggle like animated dolls. All the same. Can you imagine one of them as Empress? Mother would have the poor girl for breakfast, while I go away to fight in the next war."

"We are at peace. Except for your uncle's foolish obsession with the city of Dean, there are no battles left to fight, boy," Yun snapped. "Sheath your sword. Preferably in your willing wife. One who can give you sons."

"So that in time, I will have this discussion with my sons, as you are with me?" Yi asked with a wry smile. Obedient to his father's wishes, he slid his sword into its leather sheath at his side. "I am not ready to settle down to a life in court, where I will grow fat as all I do is waddle between my wife's bed and your chambers, to advise you or carry out whatever minor errands you think suitable. Perhaps it is time to look at expanding our borders. That I would at least be good at."

"We are at peace!" Yun exploded. "We do not make war on our neighbours. Especially not while General Li keeps most of our army occupied in the siege of Dean. We are a nation of cultured, educated, enlightened...."

"How long do you think our neighbours will leave us alone if they know the noblemen of our court spend more time on poetry than swordplay? Some of them have never fought a single opponent, let alone a battle. The last battle I fought, they ran screaming from the field at the first sign of blood, for all the world like they were girls shrieking at a spider. Your cultured, enlightened courtiers are weak, Father."

Yun took a deep breath. "I know. In a time of peace and prosperity, we have the luxury of learning to write good poetry, instead of fighting for our lives. So that they may be weak...their rulers must be strong. The Empress and I protect our people with our strength, and that of the armies who serve us. One day, you will do the same, I hope, or your sons will."

"I serve you best in the army, Father. I have no patience for court. You know that."

"In time, perhaps you will learn patience, as I did. And learn to see the value of poetry. For no warrior is forgotten when his deeds are immortalised in a ballad the people love." Yun smiled. "Perhaps that is what you need. A woman who is your complement, your opposite, your partner. While you fight, she will compose poetry so that your descendants will recount your deeds forever."

"The only partner I want is one who can oppose me when I train. I have no use for a woman, unless she holds a sword. There are tales of warrior women of old, and even the old general, Sunxi, taught a king's concubines to fight. If I can train an army, I can certainly train one woman," Yi said.

"The only sword you want your wife to hold is yours. In bed. In the past, there were warrior women. Unnatural creatures that necessity forged into fighters. Those kind of women no longer exist, Yi." Yun sighed. "But I will make a deal with you. You are still young. Go to Dean, and end the siege. General Li listens to you. Enjoy the battle while it lasts. But when it is over…you will come home. I will hold a court ball and invite every noble maiden in the kingdom, and from their number, you shall choose a bride."

"I don't want a bride," Yi said through clenched teeth.

"Is it men you prefer, then?" Yun asked. "For ancestors' sake, boy, you don't have to love the girl. Just close your eyes and imagine she is someone else, poke her a bit, and beget some sons! You must marry. I command it."

The Emperor did not issue commands to his son very often, and Yi was both a dutiful son and a loyal subject.

Yi sighed. "No, Father, I do not want a lover of any kind, male or female. I wish only to fight, for that is when I feel most alive. But if you command it, then I will obey. I will go to the siege at Dean, and when it is over, I shall return and marry whatever girl you wish."

"Whatever girl you wish, boy. You're the one who has to bed her, not me," Yun grumbled, but Yi could see his father was hiding a smile. The Emperor had gotten his way, as he always did.

At least Yi got one more campaign. And if General Li was in command, it would be a long campaign indeed. Yi wouldn't have to look at a woman again until the siege was over. Better yet, maybe his father would grow tired of waiting, and choose one of his brothers as his heir instead, leaving Yi free to command armies in the Emperor's name. Bliss, surely.

Nine

Mai rode at the head of an army, or at least she thought she did, until the city of Dean rose into view. What she saw made the troops at her back look like a troupe of travelling performers after a night of carousing. Tired, undisciplined and dirty. Mai barely noticed as the men were marched off to one of the fortified camps ringing the city around. She was too busy marvelling at the construction that had gone into besieging an entire city.

Dean itself was huge, its massive walls rising high above the surrounding plain, dwarfing the moat that seemed a mere puddle at its feet.

A second line of walls encircled the first, though

they were thinner and made of timber. Tree trunks had been cut down and their tops sharpened into spikes to make these walls, which were broken by camps and watchtowers all the way along. Too many to count. How many men did General Li have? Not enough to man all of this, surely – hence why her father's people had been called up to enlist.

This didn't match her idea of battle. That involved two armies, clashing on the plain. The clash of swords and spears and the twang of bowstrings. How did one fight a war with all these buildings?

Mai pondered the question as she surveyed the encampment. Some of the watchtowers had wheels at the bottom, and were joined in pairs by a sort of skybridge between them. They were siege towers, then, capable of being wheeled to the wall and used to help the General's troops climb into the city. They looked complete, so why had the General not employed them for their purpose? Perhaps he did not have the men.

Still, it seemed foolish to keep the siege towers on display, where they were clearly visible from the city walls. The defenders would know what was coming, and have time to plan a defensive strategy against them. The besieging army would be at a disadvantage, heading into terrain they did not know. An enclosed city, no less, where the defenders lived and knew better than anyone else could.

Now, if they could tempt the city's forces out of the gates, then the besiegers might have an advantage. But what could be tempting enough to entice them out? Perhaps…

"You're to report to General Li," the messenger said, interrupting Mai's battle plans. "I'll take you to the command tent, and then I can return to the capital. Where things are civilised."

Mai followed him into the biggest stockade, which sat on a natural rise on the otherwise flat plain. The General's tent was actually a wooden hut, built on a mound of earth in the middle of camp overlooking what appeared to be a training ground. The General himself was the only man in full armour, though he carried his helmet under his arm as he watched the troops training below.

No, not training. Sparring, Mai noticed with interest. She had not trained with an opponent since she left her father's household, and she was eager to learn to fight better against someone more skilled than she.

"This is the last one. Yeong Mao, Yeong Fu's son," the messenger announced, shoving Mai forward so that she almost overbalanced.

She righted herself before she fell at the General's feet. "My father sent me to learn the art of war, General," Mai said. "He has trained me well."

General Li snorted. "That's what they all say, right up until they turn and run in battle. Cowards. Right. Whatever-your-name-is, go join the other young noblemen down there. First, we'll see how well you can fight, and then give you something to do."

He turned to speak to one of his aides, effectively dismissing her.

The messenger seemed mesmerised by the group of young men the General had pointed to. "Good luck, Yeong Mao," he said softly.

Mai swallowed. "Thank you," she said. "I wish you a safe journey back to the capital."

She joined the circle of boys, who formed a ring around two combatants. The smaller of the two, a boy perhaps a year or two older than Mai and not much bigger, struggled to hold his wooden sword aloft, even as he gripped the hilt with both shaking hands. The other boy – more a man, Mai decided, smacked his own wooden blade against the smaller boy's sword almost lazily, sending it flying across the circle to land at Mai's feet.

Mai reached down for the sword, which felt surprisingly light in her hand. Her father's wooden blades had a metal core, weighting them much like a proper sword, but this one was all wood. She looked up, intended to offer the practice blade back to the disarmed boy, but he now lay on his belly in the dirt, begging for mercy from the bigger boy whose blade merely touched the back of the downed boy's neck.

"Next," the victor drawled, letting his foe up.

The boy scrambled out of the circle as fast as his feet could carry him.

The next challenger was built like an ox. He would have no trouble lifting the light sword, Mai thought, as he tossed it from hand to hand like it weighed nothing. Then the challenger adopted a bold stance, knees bent, facing the victor of the previous bout.

"Try that on someone your own size!" the challenger called.

The victor strode forward, his muscles bunching as he delivered his first thrust.

The challenger managed a clumsy block, but his movements were too slow. He might have the strength to fight, but he had little practice with a sword, Mai decided. The victor delivered a series of slashing blows that his opponent barely managed to block in time, until one cut made it through, tearing through the fabric of the boy's tunic.

Mai glimpsed pale flesh for a moment before the boy dropped his blade, turned tail and ran out of the circle.

"The General will put him to good use, running messages in battle!" the victor said.

A few of the boys in the circle sniggered at this, but

the laughter died quickly when they realised the man in the middle wasn't laughing. Instead, he pointed at those who had. "You, you and you. In that order. You're up next."

The boys ducked their heads in obedience, and the first one trudged across the dirt to meet his fate.

Without taking her eyes off the fight, Mai asked the boy beside her, "Who is he?"

"The Prince of Swords, Gong Ji," the boy whispered.

Gong Ji…the man's name was Rooster? Mai tried again. "Who?"

"Best swordsman in the kingdom, or so he says. No one's managed to beat him yet. The General said if we can stay on our feet for a turn of the hourglass in the ring with him, we will be assigned to his camp, and will lead troops in battle when we breach the city walls. The rest of us will go to different watchtowers to stand guard over the city."

Stand guard? There was no honour in guard duty. Leading troops into battle…if Mai wanted to earn honour for her family, then she must find a way to fight this Prince of Swords.

"How many have beaten the hourglass?" Mai asked.

The boy swallowed. "So far, none."

The Prince of Swords was a master swordsman indeed, then. An enemy she must know as well as she knew herself, for Mai to be victorious.

For the first time, she took a good look at the man, instead of his less skilled opponents. The prince lowered his head and barrelled into a boy, knocking him into the dirt. The prince was a big man, who used his size and strength to his advantage against smaller opponents like this one. He held his sword like a man who had trained for longer than Mai had, for he moved with a fluidity that spoke of experience with a good teacher. His sword truly was an extension of his arm – and a long arm, too. He used his bigger reach to attack his opponents before they had the chance to touch him, forcing them to defend against a fast flurry of blows that were designed to distract, not hit, until the prince saw an opening and took it. Not to hurt or to kill – no, he knocked his opponent down. In battle, his enemy would be trampled or run through, Mai knew. She suspected the prince did, too.

She watched him peel off his sweat-soaked tunic and use it to mop his face. Her belly sort of swirled a little, as if she was suddenly hungry for something. Strange. She'd eaten some of her travel rations only an hour ago. Why the sight of a man's muscled body made her feel hungry again, she had no idea. Yet as she stared, she realised he had an impressive collection of scars. Battle scars. The prince was a veteran of many battles, if his back was any indication. He would lead troops into battle. Perhaps he already had – many times. Now Mai's appetite took a different turn – she hungered for his knowledge and experience, so that she might lead troops to victory, too.

"Any of you other ladies want to come and dance with me?" the prince asked, turning slowly on the spot so he could meet the eyes of every boy who dared raise his gaze from the dirt. "Or will you all be standing guard on the watchtowers like the others?"

It was now or never.

Mai stepped forward. "I shall dance with you."

Ten

Even as Yi called out his final challenge to the circle of boys, he knew what their answer would be. He'd defeated too many of them for the rest to have the courage to face him. What was left were the cowards who were not fit for war. Bureaucrats who belonged in the capital, his father's new batch of aspiring poets, and…

"I will dance with you."

Yi looked up in surprise to meet the eyes of a boy he hadn't seen before. Small for his age or perhaps younger than the rest, he was hardly an impressive specimen, but he was no coward. His eyes brimmed with determination as he lifted the wooden practice sword in a fighting stance that even Yi had to admit looked convincing. The boy's small stature would be his downfall, though – he would be no match for Yi's strength, or that of an enemy soldier.

Yi considered rushing the boy, but decided to let him attack first. There was something different about this one. "I am ready," he announced, beckoning the boy to advance.

The boy stood firm and shook his head. "Where is the hourglass?" he demanded.

The forgotten timekeeper was produced and set back on its stool. Yi could feel the boy's eyes on him as he turned it and let the sand flow. "There," Yi said, moving to face the boy again.

The boy smiled, almost as though he was eager to begin. "I am ready," he said.

Yi had to admire his gall as the boy beckoned him to attack. Had he not been watching the other…well, one could hardly call them battles. Bouts, maybe. Very short ones.

"Then attack," Yi said.

The boy shook his head once more. He darted a glance at the hourglass.

Yi stifled a grin. So that was the boy's strategy. Stall until the sand ran out. If he would not attack, then Yi would.

Yi darted across the circle until he was two strides

from the boy, then ducked his head and barrelled into him.

Or he would have, except where the boy had been a moment ago, Yi met only air. His foot connected with something, hooking under it, and he pitched forward. He tried to turn it into a combat roll, but his foot was caught and he sprawled on his belly in the dirt instead.

He'd tripped. Somehow, he'd tripped on uneven ground and fallen. It could have happened to anyone.

Yi rose to his feet, scanning the ground for the unseen obstacle. All he saw was a shoe, which matched the other one the boy still wore. He'd run so fast, he'd left his shoe behind for Yi to trip over. Fortuitous.

As if the boy could read his mind, he removed his other shoe and tossed it under the stool. Now he fought barefoot.

Yi tucked the lost shoe into his pocket. "We're not through yet," he said, raising his sword. Though the boy had no more shoes to ambush him with, Yi didn't charge again. Instead, he concentrated on speed, moving the wooden blade so fast none of the other boys had had a chance to block him.

Not so this one. He blocked every blow, stepping into Yi's reach instead of out of it, giving his shorter arms the advantage until he was so close every time he blocked, the hilt of his sword tapped Yi's chest.

Yi thought little of it – what were a few bruises

from training? – until the boy slammed the hilt of his sword into Yi's solar plexus. Yi coughed, unable to breathe, but he knew it would be only temporary. He whirled away from the boy, putting space between them once more to give him time to recover.

Time he did not have. The boy harried him, trading blows every step of Yi's retreat until Yi managed to suck in another breath.

"Enough playing," Yi said sharply. He stepped forward, thinking to force the boy back with another flurry of blows, but he stood his ground. Still, he left an opening that Yi was waiting for. He bulled into the boy with his shoulder, determined to knock him into the dirt.

The boy twisted and Yi found he'd overreached. Already off balance, Yi stepped forward to right himself, but his foot caught on something again. This time, instead of falling on his face, he landed on his back, the breath knocked out of him once more. And there was no shoe in sight.

Honour forced Yi to his feet. He could not be seen lying in the dirt – not even if he was the victor of a hundred bouts today would they have any respect for him if this boy beat him. Grimly, he lifted his sword once more.

The boy held up his hand, palm out. "The hourglass is out of sand," he announced. "And I am still on my feet."

By the ancestors, so he was. Yi threw his sword in the dirt. "You boys, collect up the practice swords and put them away, then report to the General's aide for watchtower assignments." He pointed. "You, you and you will join the runners. And you." He glared at the boy who'd beaten him. "What is your name?"

The boy took his time handing his practice sword to one of the others, treating it with the respect of a real weapon and not the toy it was. Finally, he said, "My name is Yeong Mao."

"You were lucky, Yeong Mao," Yi growled. "Don't expect the enemy to trip over your lost shoe in battle. You must train, and train hard, if you want to remain in a fighting unit and not be sent to do guard duty like the others."

Mao's eyes darkened. "It was luck and skill that beat you. Or are you ashamed to admit defeat?"

He didn't seem to care that he was unarmed, or smaller than Yi. Mao took up a fighting stance once more, his hand taking the place of his blade.

This was madness. Yi didn't want some hot-headed youngster beside him in battle. He reached for one of the practice swords, determined to best this boy in the second bout. His honour was at stake.

"Do your worst," Yi spat.

This time, Mao attacked, blurring into motion so

fast Yi barely saw him until Yi lay flat on his back again, and the boy bent over him.

"I'm going to kill you," Yi wheezed, fighting to drag air into his lungs as he clambered painfully to his feet.

"I'd wager this one will be first over the walls when we attack," General Li said, clapping his hands as he strode onto the practice ground. "Well done, boy. What's your name?"

"Yeong Mao," Mao repeated.

"Yeong Fu's son?" the General mused.

Mao nodded.

"You can share a tent with Yi here. Maybe even teach him a thing or two. Looks like he's getting rusty in his old age." General Li grinned.

Old age? Li was more than twice his age, Yi fumed. As for sharing a tent with the boy… He waited until the General moved out of earshot before he muttered, "One night. You can sleep in my tent for one night, but I want a rematch in the morning. No tricks this time."

Mao bowed his head, not bothering to hide his own grin. "Gladly, Gong Ji. Any time you wish to lie in the dirt again, I will help you."

"My name is Jun Yi," Yi bit out through clenched teeth. "Get it right, boy."

"My name is Mao, not boy," Mao corrected. His eyes flashed with an anger that equalled Yi's own.

"And you are Gong Ji. A puffed-up rooster who is not as good in a fight as he thinks."

Yi lifted his fist to clout the boy, only to see his arm come up in an automatic block. Mao might be small, but he had some combat training, at least. "Tomorrow, we will test the truth of that," Yi promised. "And when I am done with you, you will be the chicken, not me, running away in fear."

Mao snorted. "We shall see."

Eleven

As Mai lay on her pallet, listening to Yi's breathing on the other side of the tent, her blood buzzed like it contained a swarm of bees. She couldn't recall ever being this angry at anyone before.

For what had felt like a perfect moment that stretched for eternity, she had stood in the ring opposite Yi in her first fight against a real opponent. And her performance had been flawless. Not even her father could have found fault with her today. The world had stood still while only she and Yi moved in it, and she had moved faster than he did every time. A deadly dance indeed.

How dare that puffed-up rooster claim her victory

was because of some dishonourable trick?

For the first time in her life, she'd tasted triumph, and a moment later he'd trodden it into the dust by suggesting she'd won because of a lucky accident.

Unlucky, more like, that when she'd hooked her leg around his to trip him, his huge, lumbering foot had dislodged her shoe. Had she fought barefoot, the result would have been the same. Perhaps she should insist that they both fight barefoot on the morrow. Or if she went shoeless, he went shirtless, for the truth was that seeing his muscles so clearly had allowed her to almost read his mind, for the muscles of his chest gave away his next move before he made it. It had been easy to counter him, with so much warning.

She half expected Yi to attack her while she lay in bed, for a man so quick to assume dishonourable behaviour in others must be less than honourable himself. That was why she gripped the hilt of her dagger, ready to use it if the need arose, but his breathing grew even, as though he slept.

She listened a while longer, until she was satisfied that the man really was asleep, before she set her shoes alongside her bed, where they would trip him up if he approached her. Her dagger went under her pillow, within easy reach should she need it during the night. Then she rolled herself up in her blanket and sank into sleep.

Twelve

The eighth time Yi picked himself up off the ground where Mao had dumped him, he resolved it would be the last. "You win," he panted, bowing to the boy.

Mao gave a curt nod. "Just like yesterday." His eyes glittered with what Yi fancied was a warning.

"Just like yesterday," Yi agreed. He knew when he was beaten, though it had been a long time since anyone had been able to do so. He'd been smaller than Mao, and probably younger, too. He had long since surpassed his training masters. Perhaps Mao's master would be willing to train him, too. "Who taught you to fight like that?"

"My father, of course," Mao said, slipping his shoes

back on his feet. The movement was oddly graceful, stirring something inside Yi that he didn't understand.

A memory, he told himself. For there was nothing about a boy putting on his shoes that could inspire any kind of feeling in him.

"And your father is Yeong Fu?" Yi asked, hoping he'd gotten the name right. It sounded vaguely familiar, but he couldn't place the man. That was strange in itself, for Yi prided himself on knowing every man at court who had some skill with a blade. A man who fought as well as Mao should be remembered. "Have I seen him at court?"

Mao shook his head. "My father is rarely at court. The last time the Emperor summoned him, I was but a small child. Too small and weak to even lift a wooden practice sword, though my father insisted otherwise."

A country noble, then, Yi guessed. Which made it all the stranger that he should know the man's name. "Did he train troops?"

Mao straightened with pride. "He trained me, just as he did all the other boys in his army, he said. He was a well-respected general who won many battles."

Not someone Yi had fought under, though. "Your father must be very old, then, if he has retired from commanding troops."

Mao opened his mouth to reply, then closed it again, as if to keep a secret from escaping. Interesting.

Finally, he said, "That is why he sent me to war in his stead." He kept his eyes firmly on the ground.

A lie, Yi assumed, or only a partial truth. No matter. General Li had them sharing a tent. Mao could hardly avoid him. Whatever secrets he kept would leak out eventually, and Yi intended to be there when they did.

"How many battles have you fought in?" Yi asked.

Mao wet his lips. "None," he admitted. "How many have you?"

"Too many to count," Yi replied easily. It was true. He didn't remember any more. He had learned that the only battles that mattered were the ones you fought at the present moment, and the next one. "If I'd fought against someone like you, though, I wouldn't have survived."

Mao's mouth dropped open. "But…trained soldiers at war…fighting is what they are trained for. Not just a little practice in the yard every morning, like me."

"There is more to army life than fighting. They spend more time digging, doing camp chores and drilling than actually fighting," Yi said. "They train daily, but as a unit. A common soldier is not a warrior, or a fine swordsman. He is but one part of a company of men, who must all do the same thing at the same time when they are ordered to do so. They move as one, not as men."

Mao nodded thoughtfully. "A well-trained army is as essential to victory as a good general, and capable officers. So my father says."

When the siege was over, Yi resolved to find Mao's father and make the man train him. If he could turn this small boy into a formidable fighter, surely he would welcome the Prince of Swords as his pupil. "But so is keeping the army well-fed. Come, I will show you the officers' mess, where you will find the worst meal you ever ate."

Mao's eyes widened. "Are we short on provisions? That does not bode well for victory."

Yi laughed. "Oh, we have provisions aplenty. You arrived at the head of a sizeable baggage train. The problem is the cooks are all army men. Just one of the palace cooks could turn every meal into a dream for your senses, but our cooks? The days when you can eat what they produce, it is a good day." It was on the tip of his tongue to say Heng, his manservant, was on good terms with the General's cook, so he rarely needed to visit the officers' mess, but Yi resisted. Let Mao learn what it really meant to serve in the army, instead of training at home with his father. The boy could surely fight, but something told Yi that he was too soft for army life. He still might turn and run in battle, like all the other noble boys he'd fought yesterday. Yi would take the city with seasoned fighting men, not boys. And young Mao was not a man yet. Though he might become one before Li ended the siege, at the snail's pace he worked at.

No matter. That would give him more time to win Mao over, so that his father would agree to train him.

Thirteen

Perhaps Yi was not so bad after all, Mai mused as she forced down another mouthful of bland food. She couldn't keep the smile off her face after what she felt was a fantastic training session that morning. Yi had fought hard, but she had fought harder, and victory was sweet once more. Especially when the man acknowledged it this time.

She had made some mistakes, she admitted, but Yi had not been quick enough to capitalise on them. On the morrow, she would improve.

In the meantime, she listened to Yi's tales of battles he had fought in. More than her father had, to hear the man talk. She had heard every story her father could tell more times than she could count, but Yi's were all new. Some were even fought here, on this very plain, on the rare occasions General Li had tempted the city's troops out to do battle. Those were fewer now the walls were up, but Yi admitted the city's army still ventured out to test Li's defences. It had been weeks since their last sortie – perhaps Mao would be lucky enough to join the next battle, Yi said.

It took Mai a moment to remember that the name was hers, but it was close enough to her own that she hoped she would soon grow used to it.

"We'll have plenty of poets to immortalise it, when you do get to fight," he said, laughing.

Poets? "What do you mean?"

He jerked his chin at the nearest watchtower. "Remember all those boys yesterday I sent to do guard duty?"

She nodded.

"Noble youths from court, most of them. Their fathers want them to serve in the army, but fighting is out of favour in my father's court. He favours poetry, and so do most of them. They might not know one end of a sword from another, but they are familiar with a calligraphy brush. I gave them the best vantage points to see whatever may come, and their best chance of surviving to tell the tale when they return to court."

Mai frowned. "So you deny them the honour of dying in the Emperor's service, when that is why they are here?"

"There is honour in dying well in battle, but there is none when you die screaming, running from the battlefield like a pig fleeing slaughter. Honour is not earned through throwing away your life." He pointed at the common soldiers' camp below them. "If they fall in battle, it will be hard fought. They have entered the Emperor's service and trained every day for battle. But a boy who knows nothing of fighting, who has not trained a day in his life? They will be slaughtered, with no honour on either side."

Finally, Mai understood. Perhaps her desire to honour her ancestors by dying in battle would be a bad idea. She liked living, and if there was another way… "Why didn't you train them? The great Sunxi trained concubines to fight. Surely boys of the right age…"

Yi shook his head. "Not all men are born to fight, just as not all women are born to serve. Some choose a different path, or destiny chooses it for them." He laughed. "For those boys, I chose their path. One which has a future for them, and won't get me killed in battle as they run in fear at the first sight of blood. You'd better not turn out to be like them, Mao, or I'll find you a watchtower, too."

Mai laughed. "You tell tales of all the battles you

have fought, but after fighting against you, I wonder that you survived at all. You're more likely to get yourself killed than anything I could do. Some fighter you are, Rooster."

It was Yi's turn to frown. "Will you stop calling me that?"

She leaned forward. "I shall stop calling you that when you are no longer a rooster. Beat me in a fight, and I will address you as your Highness, Prince of Swords, the best hero and fighter there ever was. Until then...I think I shall keep pulling your pretty tail feathers."

"Then another rematch on the morrow," Yi swore.

Mai inclined her head. "I look forward to it."

Fourteen

Weeks passed, every day the same as the last. Mai and Yi would begin the day with a new bout, and she would proceed to drop him on his back or his front or occasionally even his head until he cried enough for one day and sulkily slunk off to find breakfast. Sometimes, they would join the regular army in their training exercises, but at others, the General sent them on errands to the other camps.

The garrison inside Dean led sorties out to attack some of the camps at night, stealing their supplies and burning what they could, before sneaking back into the city. She'd seen the smoking aftermath of these raids, and occasionally witnessed a battalion marching out to help the camp while they were under attack, but no battle seemed to be in the General's plans. Yi believed the General's strategy was to wait here until the city starved, which would take a very long time with the city stealing their supplies to supplement their own. This kind of war seemed a very tedious business. So much for a campaign being as swift as the wind. Sure, the General might stand as firm as a mountain, but he moved more like a snail than a thunderbolt, and the only plundering going on was by the citizens of Dean, who understood the qualities of fire all too well, for they used it to great effect.

Many times, Mai found herself shaking her head. The commander of Dean evidently knew the art of war intimately, but the General did not. She began to wonder if her father was right, and whether Dean was the side that should win. After all, the better commander with the better army and the better terrain and all the supplies they needed would surely be victorious. She didn't dare mention that to Yi, though. Bad enough that her father might be a traitor, without letting the Emperor's son know she might be one, too.

She still slept with a knife under her pillow, but she now knew Yi well enough to be sure she'd never use it. For all his pride, he was an honourable man. And a protector of poets. If he wanted to kill her, he would do so in a fair fight, not in the darkness while she slept.

The food alternated between bland, awful and burned, but it was mostly edible, so she bit back her complaints until she realised no one else was. Men whined more than Jing when they didn't like their food, she found.

She had to admit she didn't mind army life. Her mother had grown up with it, first with her father, and then with her husband, so it made sense that Mai would take to it as naturally as a duck to water.

Oh, duck. Mai's mouth watered at the thought of eating one that had been cooked properly, instead of the tough old bird the cooks had produced yesterday.

Gradually, she became known around the camp. Most of the men were too young to have served under her father, but they had grown up hearing the stories about him. One man even asked her if she'd do the honour of crossing swords with him in the training ring, if only so that he could tell his children he had fought with Yeong Fu's son.

Mai could not refuse him, so she told him to meet her after the next day's bout with Yi.

Somehow, word spread, so that when she and Yi arrived for yet another rematch, there must have been more than fifty men milling around, forming a crowd around the ring so that she could not even see the sand as she approached.

"What's this?" Yi asked irritably.

Several men turned, and all of them bowed at the sight of the prince. Yi's name was on everyone's lips, along with Mai's father's.

The man she'd met only yesterday stepped forward. "Yeong Mao. Your Highness." He bowed. "When I told the others, they asked to come and watch. Some asked whether they, too, might have the honour of crossing swords with one or even both of you."

"Both?" The idea intrigued Mai. She had never fought at someone's side before.

Yi came to her rescue. "In my grandfather's day, he held tournaments where there was an event called a melee. There are two teams of men, and only one can emerge victorious. They fight together, like companies of opposing armies. Toward the end of the event, when many are injured, a winning team of two or three men have fought back to back until there is no one else left standing." He seemed to be struggling with something, but finally he added, "I cannot imagine a better fighter than yourself to have at my back in a melee. What do you say we postpone our rematch?"

Mai agreed. She listened while Yi laid down the rules, before she found her back pressed up against the warm wall of muscle that was Yi. She'd never been this close to a man before, and she rather liked it. Right up until she realised she had two soldiers rushing toward her, armed with wooden practice swords and more enthusiasm than anyone should have this early in the morning.

The fight. Of course. That's where her mind should be, she scolded herself. Not on the handsome man at her back whose behind kept rubbing against hers.

The sun was well up by the time Yi breathlessly called a halt to the mock battle. Bruised but exhilarated, Mai couldn't keep the smile off her face.

Yi used the hem of his robe to wipe the sweat from his forehead. "What did you think of that, boy? It's as close to battle as you'll get short of the real thing. Do you think you're man enough for more?"

Mai laughed in delight. "I want to do it again tomorrow, and the next day, too."

Yi stared at her. "You jest."

She shook her head. "Didn't you enjoy the challenge? So many different styles of fighting, so many different opponents, each thinking and acting differently so that you could lose yourself in a dance so complex you must rely on instinct and training and…" She sighed happily. "I was born for this."

"You're crazy," Yi said instead.

Mai laughed again. "Perhaps I am."

"A man as crazy as you needs breakfast. Shall we see what the cooks have burned for us today?"

For the first time, instead of stalking off in a huff, Yi joined her for breakfast. It would not be the last time, either.

Fifteen

Yi held still while Heng, his manservant, shaved him. Heng's hands were perfectly steady, but that didn't change the fact that he held a sharp blade very close to Yi's face. One slip could be disastrous.

"I don't know how you can let a man hold a blade to your throat without defending yourself," Mao commented as he bundled his clothing into a sheet from his bed. "If anyone got that close to me with a knife, I'd automatically block and disarm him."

Yi wanted to shake his head but he managed to resist. Heng wasn't done yet. "It's a matter of loyalty and trust. Heng and I have campaigned together for a long time. I've killed men who tried to attack him, so he's not going to kill me. I'm useful."

Heng snorted. "Enemy soldiers see him as a target. Stick near him. No one will bother to attack you, because they see him as a giant trophy they want to take home." He eyed Mao. "My family is noble like yours, but our lands are so small, there was nothing left for a younger son like me. As long as he's around, he makes life interesting. Sometimes campaigning, sometimes in court. It beats ploughing my father's fields with the villagers."

Mao nodded as if he understood.

"Are you a younger son, too?" Yi asked.

Mao laughed. "No, I am my father's firstborn. But I understand the desire to have more to my life than dreary days in a rural village. Ah, but a village does have one advantage." He bundled the sheet into a sack for his clothing and lifted it into the air. "I know who the washerwomen are, and where to find them. Here, I fear I might have to wash my own clothes in the river next time I bathe."

"Give them to Heng. He can take them and mine, too, before he fetches our breakfast," Yi said.

Heng faked a happy grin. "See, what did I tell you? Life is always interesting. Today, I become a washerwoman. Wait until some drunken soldier tries to find out what I keep under my skirts."

Yi laughed as Heng grabbed the bundle of clothing

and sashayed out, hips swaying like a prostitute touting for business.

"He does a good job at shaving, you know," Yi said when Heng was gone. "Any time you want his help, just ask. For we are friends now, are we not?"

"Yes, we are friends," Mao admitted, "but I still feel strange ordering a man about. Maybe for a prince it is different, with so many servants in the palace, but at home, it was not like that. And I mean it about the blade. My father trained me too well. If I reacted as my training tells me to, I might hurt Heng without meaning to. I don't think we would remain friends after that."

Yi laughed, but he understood. He itched for battle, too. A siege like this was frustrating.

Sixteen

A commotion in the camp outside roused Mai from a deep sleep.

"Hurry, Mao, or we'll miss it," she heard Yi say. Something heavy landed on her midsection, and her breath whooshed out of her lungs at the impact. "Get your armour on!"

With Heng's help, Mai managed to don her armour, for Yi was already geared for war, capering around the tent like a court fool. She was still buckling on her sword belt when Yi dragged her from the tent.

"What's going on?" she mumbled, fumbling with the buckle.

"Another raid on the blockade. This time, we're

sending reinforcements. We get to fight!"

Yi seemed ghoulishly excited about going out to kill other men. Mai wondered if he might be crazy after all. They joined the column of troops marching toward the city, which was lit by the orange light of flames licking toward the stars at a camp just north of their own.

When they reached the camp, Yi grabbed her arm and pulled her away from the other soldiers. "This way."

Screams erupted from the camp gates as the flames leaped higher.

Mai wasn't sure whether to run toward the sound or away from it. "What's happening?"

"They brought fire lances," Yi said. They rounded a section of wall and found the next section had been burned to ash, leaving them a clear view into the camp and the massacre at the gate. "Big bamboo tubes that explode and take down whole sections of wall, like this one, or many men all at once."

Mai's stomach churned. This was not the sort of fighting her father had taught her. She pointed at a box four men were wheeling toward the gate. "What is that?"

Yi stared intently in the direction she was pointing. "A cart, I think. I don't – "

A great gout of flame erupted from a pipe on top

of the cart, dousing everything in its path in fire.

Mai looked on in horror as men caught in it screamed, then fell to the ground, writhing as they burned. Whatever the box was, it was monstrous.

"First fire lances, now fierce fire oil, and a box that sprays it," Yi said, awed. "So that's why the General has not attacked. If they're willing to risk one of these in a raid, they must have many more. All along the walls, ready to burn anyone and anything that comes close to the city."

"Not just ready to do it. It's doing it now!" Mai snapped, charging toward the box.

"What are you doing? They'll kill you!" Yi hissed.

"Not if I get to them first," Mai said grimly. She took the first man low in the gut, knocking him over so that his head hit the wheel of the cart, rendering him unconscious. Second, she tripped the man directing the nozzle spitting flames. The liquid spilled over his clothes instead, and Mai had to back away in a hurry as he became a flaming torch.

A third man stopped working the pump to stare at his fiery compatriot, so he didn't even see Mai's kick coming. He was unconscious before he hit the ground. Mai turned to deal with the fourth operator of the deadly box, only to find Yi extracting his sword from the man's belly.

"Your first battle, and you kill three men in the time

it takes me to kill one. Did one of your ancestors sleep with a barbarian war god or something?" Yi asked.

"I didn't kill anyone," Mai defended herself. "Those two are just unconscious and that one set fire to himself."

"You'll be everyone's hero tonight," Yi muttered, before raising his voice. "This camp belongs to the Emperor, and anyone who is not loyal to him will burn like a torch!" he roared.

"It's the Prince of Swords! He holds the fire machine!" someone shouted.

Mai drew her sword as a group of men rushed toward them, only to recognise them as General Li's men.

"They're running back to hide in Dean now," another man said. "Look at them go!"

In the light of the still burning barricade, Mai could see men streaming back into a small city gate, before they barred it behind them.

Cheering erupted around Yi and Mai.

Mai couldn't understand it. She could still smell fuel and burning flesh, and there were corpses underfoot. What was there to cheer about? Men had died here.

Yi slung a comradely arm around Mai's shoulder. "I bet you feel like a big man now, your first battle and all." He looked just as deliriously happy as the others.

Mai couldn't seem to find the words to express the

horror and guilt and sheer desolation she felt right now, so she just nodded and let Yi take her back to their camp while the others cleaned up what was left of this one.

Seventeen

By dusk of the next day, the wrecked camp looked almost as good as new, with the walls replaced already. A large barracks tent had become a hospital, filled with piteous groans from those who'd survived the burning touch of the flamethrowing machine or one of the fire lances. There were a lot of men not in the hospital, though, who seemed to be drinking everything in sight, but they raised their cups to toast Mai whenever they saw her. It seemed that Yi had spread the story that she'd disabled the flamethrower, and they looked at her like she was some kind of hero.

A hero who wouldn't be able to sleep tonight without having nightmares about the man she burned alive by accident. Already, she saw him whenever she closed her eyes, and his screams still rang in her ears, though they had only lasted a few seconds before the flames had silenced him forever.

For the first time, she noticed women roaming around the camp, instead of in their own little enclave on the far side of the cookfires. Mai knew they were camp followers, the women who served the army in various capacities in times of war. Not all of them were prostitutes. Some of them were soldiers' wives, like her mother had been, but the women she saw now made it clear they were not married…yet.

After seeing a steady succession of swaying hips, batted eyelashes and blown kisses as the women walked past her, she turned to find Yi grinning beside her. "So which one do you like?" he asked.

"I'm not in the market for a wife," Mai grumbled, picking at her tasteless dinner.

Yi laughed. "Not a wife. Just one night. After your first battle, it's tradition to take a woman. You being such a hero and all, they all want that honour. If you don't pick soon, the other men will get impatient and the best ones will be busy."

"It's the first battle for all of them?" Mai asked. When Yi laughed even louder, she wished she hadn't said anything.

"Of course not, but can you blame them? Men died

today, and when you remind a man of his mortality, he remembers what he likes most in life. Good food, and the company of a good woman." Yi took a mouthful of his food and grimaced. "When all we have is women, and willing ones at that…well, why not?"

Mai could think of half a dozen answers to that, none of which she wanted to tell him. As if to illustrate her point, one woman climbed into the lap of a man sitting not far from them, pushed his chest until he lay down flat, and began riding him like a horse. "What does she think she's doing?" Mai muttered.

Yi stared at her. "You've never had a woman before."

Of course not, Mai wanted to say, but knew she couldn't. "Have you?" she asked instead.

"Of course," Yi said. "My first battle was a long time ago, and when I was younger…" He trailed off, then cleared his throat and began again. "But it is different for me. I am the Emperor's son, my children will have royal blood no matter who their mother is. A bastard child could make trouble for my family's succession. Not something you need to worry about, though. You should enjoy tonight."

"All I want to do is sleep," Mai said, watching several more couples start rutting, as if they didn't care who saw them. Perhaps they didn't.

"Mao – " Yi reached for her, but Mai shrugged

away from his grasp.

"Enjoy celebrating this victory. I'm sure there will be many more," she said, loud enough for the other men to hear her. A ragged cheer rose up, the sound following her all the way back to her tent.

The sounds of celebration continued long into the night, but her heart was heavy. Men had died because of her, and because of the strange box that now sat in the camp outside her tent. As long as these things existed, there could be no victory, for too many men would die in the most horrible of ways.

By the time the sun rose, Mai had not slept, but she had thought of many ways in which the boxes might be destroyed. Most would not work, but she only needed one that would.

She staggered out of the tent. Half a dozen men, looking much like she felt, stared back at her. Including Yi and Heng.

"Good morning, Sleeping Beauty," Yi greeted her.

Mai took that to mean she looked worse than the hungover men beside him. "It will be if we have a fire lance, and someone who knows how to use it," she said.

Yi frowned. "Why?"

Mai jerked her head toward the flamethrower. "Help me take that to an empty field and I'll show you."

Eighteen

It took four fire lances before one managed to hit its target. The results were better than anything Yi could have expected, though. The explosive ball landed on top of the cart, blossoming into an orange flower that ignited the liquid pooled on the cart beneath it. Yi held his breath as the pool caught fire. A loud boom made him duck for cover as a wave of heat blasted over their hastily dug earth rampart. When Yi dared to raise his head above the rampart, there was nothing left to see except some twisted pieces of metal where the cart had once been.

Yi seized Mao's arm. "That's it! The way to break the siege. You must tell the General." He hauled the boy to his feet, and pulled him toward the General's house.

Mao resisted. "I am inexperienced in war. Surely the General knows all this already."

"If he did, he would have attacked and the siege would be over. He's a fool who might know how to train men, but he is lost when it comes to war. But you…you see things so clearly you were born for battle. To command troops in battle. To victory. More than Li, or even me."

Mao turned bright red. Evidently the boy was not used to praise. "You're mistaken. I'm not…"

"You are." Yi marched Mao to the General's house and shoved him through the open doorway.

As Yi had expected, a strategy session was underway.

"What is it?" Li asked irritably. "We are in the middle of a strategy meeting. Whatever the boy has done, it can wait. Or discipline him yourself."

"General, Mao has done nothing wrong. He says you are wrong about the city's defences. You must listen to what this boy has to say," Yi insisted.

"Who are you to criticise the General?" General Li boomed, annoyed.

"I'm Yeong Mao, sir," Mao said. "My parents were Yeong Fu and Da Ying. I have studied the art of war all my life. My mother insisted upon it."

Da Ying? Yi's ears pricked up at that name. Of all the warrior women he'd heard of, Da Ying was the most legendary of the lot. A general's daughter, she'd married a junior officer and helped him through victory after victory until he rose to the rank of general. Then, she went into combat beside him. Yi had heard a tale about how her husband had fallen in battle, so she commanded the army in his stead, all the while carrying his unconscious body on her back. He itched to ask Mao if the story was true. And if he had any sisters. If he had to marry, a daughter of Da Ying might be his best chance of finding a woman he could tolerate.

"Well, then, Yeong Mao. Tell me what I am wrong about." There was a dangerous edge to Li's tone.

Mao evidently caught it, too. "It's not that you are wrong, sir. Those are Jun Yi's words, not mine. I merely made a remark about the fire lances and flamethrowers, and how they might be turned against the city."

General Li rose to his feet. "How?" he demanded.

For the first time, Mao seemed afraid. "Well, they are hollow, their tanks filled with explosive material. The one at the skirmish this week was a tank of liquid, which caught fire once sparked. The ones on the walls are filled with projectiles, like those you fire from a trebuchet. If you were to ignite the fuel before they could fire, then they would explode, burning away whatever fuel was inside them and rendering them harmless to us. If we took them out all at once, we might even set fire to the city, driving the people out through the gates. It would be an almost bloodless victory, sir."

General Li's eyes narrowed, but then he seemed to relax. "And how do you propose we set fire to them? We just climb over the walls and sneak into the city, hoping their troops are so poorly trained they don't see us or our flaming torches as we set their city on fire?" He laughed at his own joke.

Mao's gaze hardened. "I see no reason to fight inside the city at all. Why enter terrain so familiar to them when we can flush them out to the battle ground of our choosing? We can send flaming missiles over the walls. Your trebuchet operators will need to know their range perfectly, because they must all act at once in order to create sufficient panic in the city that the city troops will not regroup. We attack their strategy. That is how we can win."

General Li's eyes widened. "If we knew the location of all their fire weapons, that might work. But we do not."

"We would know if we could get a few men inside the city, who could then send that information back to you." Mao wet his lips. "I believe I know how to sneak in without anyone seeing me. If I can mark the locations of all the lances in the city, your men could pick them off easily."

Yi's heart jumped into his throat. "The two of us will go," he said. The thought of Mao alone in the city, where anything could happen to him…

Li slammed both hands down on the table. "Yes. Yi, you take the boy into the city. I will command our troops outside and lead them to victory."

It was on the tip of Yi's tongue to refuse. Left alone our here to his own devices, Li would surely lead his army to nothing but defeat. They were good men who didn't deserve to die in a bungled battle. But he couldn't let Mao go off alone, either.

"Yes, sir," Yi found himself saying.

The rest of the meeting passed in a blur, where Li described details that Yi knew he wouldn't remember. Not that it mattered. He and Mao would be inside the city, not preparing to attack it.

It wasn't until the General dismissed them that Yi found Mao tugging him aside. When they were out of earshot of everyone else, Mao hissed, "What were you thinking? How do you expect me to get both of us into the city? You stride around like you own the world – no one will think you are some lowly worker, if you even make it inside the walls! You should have let me go alone."

Yi glanced down, to find Mao's hand still firmly gripping his arm. His skin tingled under the boy's fingers in a way that wasn't at all unpleasant. Why, if the boy had been a girl, Yi might almost...

Yi shook his head. He didn't want to kiss Mao. He wanted to keep him safe. "I know more about the city than you do. I have been inside, on many occasions. They weren't always hostile to the Emperor. Two of us can watch out for each other. It is no harder to get two men than one inside the city. It is not as though we were ten in full armour. Besides, your plan involves us either sneaking out of the city – much harder than sneaking in, as you've already mentioned – or shooting an arrow from the walls all the way to one of the camps. You are a formidable fighter, but you don't have the strength to draw a big enough bow. I do."

Mao's eyes bored into Yi's, weighing his soul, or so it seemed. Finally, he said, "All right, Rooster. You will watch my back, and I will watch yours. You will fire the message arrow if we must. Together, we will find the fire lances and the flamethrowers and end this war."

And then, Yi would be obedient to the Emperor's wishes. He would attend whatever court functions the Emperor chose to hold, and end in choosing one of Mao's sisters as his bride, and travel home with Mao to negotiate the marriage with the girl's father. As Mao's friend and future brother in law, the man could hardly refuse to train him. Yi truly would be the best swordsman in the kingdom. All thanks to Mao.

Nineteen

Mai tried to still the butterflies tumbling around in her belly as Heng helped her into her armour, but it was no use. The leather settled with a heavy layer of dread on her shoulders. Mai closed her eyes, forcing her breathing to become calm. This was no more difficult than taking a stroll into the village near her father's house. She would look like one of the people of Dean, not a spy come to conquer their city by stealth.

Yi, on the other hand, looked every bit the proud rooster today. He didn't share her nerves – in fact, he looked excited about the coming battle, though they might arrive too late to be a part of it.

"When we leave, I want you to ride for the capital

and see that letter is delivered to my father," Yi said, pointing at scroll on the table he'd spent half the night hunched over.

"Is it a final letter to your father, in case you fall in battle?" Mai asked, suddenly wishing she had spent the night writing one, too. She could die today, and she had never said goodbye to her father. Would she ever see him again?

Yi laughed. "No. This is a stroll into the city, not a battle. I wrote to tell my father that the siege will soon be over, thanks to you, and to prepare for our triumphant return to the capital. If I know him, and I do, he will hold a ball with much dancing, so that I might choose a bride from among the girls. I daresay the girls will try to capture your heart as much as they reach for mine. After all, you will be the hero of the siege of Dean. I will make sure of it. You will have your choice of any woman you want." His gaze grew wistful.

Yi had already chosen his bride, Mai guessed, for not many daydreamed without something to inspire such dreams. She might play at being a man, but she was under no illusion that such a lie would survive the marriage bed. No woman would have her, and no man either, if her stepmother was to be believed. That left her…no one.

If she died today, no one would mourn her. But if

she died with honour, the ancestors would welcome her spirit. Perhaps that was all the future Mai could hope for.

The butterflies fluttered to a halt, stilled by her sombre thoughts. Heng's arms encircled her waist, buckling on her sword. Mai closed her eyes again, imagining for a moment that the arms were Yi's. Bliss, surely, but not for her. No, she would never be a bride, let alone his. The most she could do was fight at his side and perhaps die in his arms. Not such a bad fate.

Yi could not die in the city, though. She would find a way to get him out, even if she could not. Perhaps one of his watchtower poets would sing songs about her when the war was over.

Mai threw a coarse robe over the whole ensemble, tucking her hair into a cloth cap, which turned her from a soldier girded for war into a humble peasant, collecting hay or timber to take back inside the city. They'd all seen the work parties in the no man's land between the city walls and General Li's blockade, but the besiegers paid no attention to the men who foraged for such things every other day. They were the lowest of the low in the city, and beneath the notice of superior soldiers. Except for Mai, of course, who noticed that they left the city through one of the smaller gates, where armed guards stood inside waiting, but the guards never looked at the men's faces. Their attention was for General Li's soldiers.

Today, when the peasants sallied forth from the city, then spread out across the weed-choked plain, Yi and Mai joined them, keeping their heads bowed as they collected the dried weeds and stuffed them in a sack.

The monotonous work made Yi restless, and more than once Mai noticed him losing his humble pose to survey his surroundings, like no peasant would in the presence of his betters. She hissed at him to get back to work.

Finally, she heard distant shouts and thumps from the other side of the city. The gate guards heard it, too, beckoning the cityfolk back inside, quickly, before they shut the gate. Mai broke into a run, hearing Yi's heavy footfalls hot on her heels, as she fell in with the other men. They hustled into the city, and the gate was barred behind them.

No one stopped to even look at her face, or Yi's – as Mai made her way deeper into the city. Her plan had worked. They were in.

Twenty

General Li's diversion, throwing stones over the wall with trebuchets to give his men practice for the flaming assault in the near future, lasted for a little over an hour. More than long enough for Yi and Mai to ascertain how well guarded every gate was in the city walls. They found a house a few streets in, falling down from neglect, that might do for shelter for the night, if they were forced to stay inside the city.

Several hours later, when the guards' vigilance showed no signs of lessening, Yi lay on the dirt floor beside the tiny fire, sketching a map of the city and every fire lance and flamethrower they'd found. Mao had pointed out what he thought was a fuel storage hut, for he'd glimpsed jars that resembled those the soldiers used to refuel the flamethrowers on the walls. Dutifully, Yi added that to his map as well. Destroying the fuel stores would be as helpful as destroying the weapons as well.

When he was finished, he copied the map three times, then bound each sheet of paper tightly around an arrow. Four arrows with maps – surely one would make its way back to General Li.

He took first watch while Mao slept beside him on the dirt floor. Yi resolved to do whatever it took to get the boy out of the city on the morrow. The chaos of a burning city was no place for him. No man could fight a panicked mob, and Mao would be trampled far too easily. No, they would wait for tomorrow's diversion, send the arrows toward their target, and find a way back outside.

Yi stared down tenderly at the boy. He had many brothers, but none he cared about quite as much as he did for Mao. Was it because they had fought together so much? he pondered. Perhaps. Or maybe it was something about Mao himself. For all his fighting skill, there was a softness about him that Yi did not understand.

Mao woke him at dawn, when they both knew Li would start looking for them. They stripped off their peasant garb and climbed the walls, bows in hand, when the city rang the bells to signify a call to arms. Li had placed a platoon of soldiers near the gate where they'd entered, who seemed intent on breaking through the gate, too.

Yi shook his head, not sure whether the assault was serious or yet another distraction on Li's part. Never mind. He took aim at their shields, imagining himself at target practice in camp. Each red-feathered arrow found its mark, and were embedded deeply enough in the hide not to be easily dislodged. With luck, at least one of them would make it back to camp.

After some time, the much-reduced platoon retreated back behind the blockade, dragging their injured comrades with them. Yi counted at least three red-fletched arrows among the party, and breathed a sigh of relief. Even if they couldn't make it out before the true assault on the city started, he and Mao could hole up in the falling down house until the gates opened. They had enough food for a day or two, before they would need to find some more.

On their way down from the walls, they were accosted by a hawker, who grilled skewers of meat and vegetables over a brazier. Anything was better than their rations. Yi paid for two servings of the stuff, handing one to Mao. It was the best thing he'd tasted in weeks, and it looked like Mao agreed.

No wonder Dean held out so long against the siege.

When they were so well-provisioned, they had little to lose.

In the shadow of a supply hut near one of the smaller gates, he and Mao sat down to enjoy their lunch. Yi, who had taken the lion's share of the watch the previous night, dozed off.

Mao roughly shook him awake what felt like only a moment later, but must have been hours, given how much the noon shadows had lengthened in that time. The boy's eyes were wide with panic. "They're attacking again. And this time, they have fire."

Yi jumped to his feet, fully alert. "Li wasn't supposed to attack until morning. What is he thinking?"

Mao shook his head grimly. "I don't know. He surely can't mean to fight through the night. That would be – "

Something big and orange came sailing over the wall, filling the air with searing heat. Then the whole world exploded.

Twenty-One

For a rooster, Yi sure was heavy, Mai grumbled to herself as she shoved him off her. She'd slammed into the city wall, thrown by the explosion as Li's flaming missile hit the fuel storage hut that now no longer existed. The smell of scorched flesh reached her nose and Mai gagged. Only then did she notice that some of the fuel had landed on Yi's armour, where it still burned. She tried rolling him along the ground to extinguish the flames, but it was no use. Finally, she stripped his armour off him, but the damage was done. His back was a bloody mess that only the healers could take care of. She had to get him back to camp.

Another missile landed on the wall overhead,

sending out a splash of orange light as it engulfed one of the fire lances. She had to move quickly, or both she and Yi might become casualties of General Li.

Mai took a deep breath. There was only one way she could get Yi out of there. It took all her strength to heave him onto her shoulders, and even then she staggered under his weight. But she had to get him out.

Step by agonising step, she made her way to the nearest gate. A small side gate, barely wide enough for one person to walk through, it had been left unguarded while men rushed around, attempting to put out the fires, even as Li's missiles lit more.

Mai kicked at the bar, knowing that if she set Yi down, she'd never manage to lift him again. She inched the bar up for what felt like an eternity until finally it rose above the brackets that held it, unlocking the gate. She managed to get the gate half open before she was nearly trampled by a platoon of Li's soldiers, who had been battering at the gate in an attempt to get in. She flattened herself against the wall as they trooped past her, ignoring both her and Yi until she recognised the soldiers who had first asked to join her and Yi in their morning sparring sessions.

"Min!" she gasped out. "The Prince of Swords is injured. Help me get him back to camp."

Min stopped and stared, but after a moment, he nodded and halted the flow of troops into the city so

Mai could carry Yi out. Min led the way back to the blockade, where a temporary hospital had already been set up.

Mai cried out in relief as Yi's weight was taken from her and transferred to a bed. Healers converged on him, cutting away his clothes from his ruined back as they argued on how best to treat the burns.

"What happened?" someone asked Mai.

"We were inside the city when one of the General's thunderbolt balls hit the fuel storage hut. He shielded me from the blast, which set fire to his armour. I couldn't put out the flames, so I took his armour off," Mai said, waving her hands.

"And burned yourself in the process," the healer said. "Just look at those hands. You sit right here, and I'll fetch some salve for them. It might not help him, but those are going to hurt."

Might not…? The healers might not be able to help Yi? Mai's heart constricted in her chest. They had to save him. She'd carried him out on her back to find someone who could save him. He couldn't die now. Not after all that.

"Save him first," she blurted out, dragging her stool over to his bedside. "Nothing matters more than the prince. You have to save him."

"We will," the healer soothed, smoothing something smelly over her hands. "You just sit there and watch. We'll do everything we can for him, but we won't know how badly he is hurt until he wakes up. If he wakes up."

If?

Mai couldn't even consider the possibility that Yi wouldn't wake up. He'd been hurt trying to save her from the blast. She owed him her life. "He will," she said fiercely. "And when he does, I will be here beside him to tell him the news of our victory over Dean."

"Has the General won already?" the healer asked, as calmly as though he was asking about the weather.

"I do not know," Mai replied. "But if he is not victorious, the Emperor will not forgive his failure. For losing the prince would be too high a price for anything less than a complete victory. If you see General Li, you tell him. His strategy has put Prince Yi in hospital."

"The General never visits us here. If he is unwell, he sends for a healer to his tent, not the other way around. And speaking of healing, those hands of yours will need more than salve. I'm going to bandage them up and mix you a draught for the pain. You'll be staying here tonight."

"Until he wakes, I will stay anyway. Do what you must," Mai said, gritting her teeth as even the brush of bandages against her tender skin hurt. Nevertheless, she endured it. She drank the cup of foul-tasting tea and settled down to wait.

Twenty-Two

Yi sank into his favourite dream. The one where he was victorious from his latest battle, and he lay in the arms of his bride, a woman whose softness and curves were his alone to caress. When she moaned in pleasure, her voice was low and husky – none of the high-pitched, childish giggling so popular among court ladies. He would happily spend every night devoted to bringing her joy, if only to hear her voice. Yet she was no shy, delicate doll – oh, no. She had all the brazenness of a camp follower as she returned his attentions in equal measure. His scars earned him kisses, not disgust, like they would from court ladies who preferred their men as pretty as themselves. A real woman for a real man – that was what he craved. Surely such a woman existed. He had to find her, because a lifetime of searching was worth it for even a single night of bliss in her arms.

A woman whose face he had never seen.

In the dream, his sight cleared, and once again, he beheld not a woman, but Mao's face.

Yi jerked awake, cursing. Why the boy had to invade his dreams like that, he did not know. If he married one of Mao's sisters, he would demand Mao leave them alone on their wedding night. And every other night, come to think of it.

Mao lay on the next pallet, fast asleep. It took Yi a moment to realise he could see far more clearly than usual, and the tent was bigger and noisier, too.

"What the – " he began, sitting up to take in his surroundings properly.

One of the big barracks tents had been turned into a hospital, which was full of wounded men. Why was he there, then? He wasn't wounded. The last thing he could remember was eating lunch with Mao inside Dean when General Li had attacked the city earlier than planned.

And the fuel storage hut had exploded.

Mao was here, in bed. Was he injured?

"Mao, wake up," Yi said urgently, reaching over to shake the boy. "Mao!"

When the boy didn't immediately wake, Yi shouted for a healer.

A harassed-looking healer hurried over, hushing him. "You should lie right back down, or you'll make me have to bandage you again. I'll give you a sleeping draught like I did him. You're not the only patient here, you know!"

A sleeping draught. No wonder Mao wouldn't wake. Yi released him. "Is he injured?" Yi demanded.

"He burned his hands, trying to save you," the healer said. "It will hurt some, but he won't scar as bad as you. What did you do? Mistake a flamethrower for your bed?"

"I…" Yi couldn't remember. There had been the explosion, then everything went dark. "I don't know. Did he tell you?"

"He carried you in here, shouting for a healer. Looks like you took a blast to the back. That stuff even burns armour. I didn't believe it at first, until I saw the evidence with my own eyes. You two are the only burned ones, though. Seems the General has done something right this time." The healer nodded.

No, he hadn't. General Li had attacked early, Yi fumed. He and Mao should have been well out of the city before he launched the attack. Instead, they'd been caught in the middle of it and Mao…

Yi tried to swallow down the lump in his throat.

The very thought that the boy had been hurt by Li's bungling cut him to the core. Li would not get away with this.

Yi rose, laying a hand on the healer's shoulder to steady myself. "I must speak with the General."

The healer shook his head. "You're not leaving this hospital in that condition. You need to get back into bed."

Yi bristled. "Who are you to give the Emperor's son orders? I will go where I wish, healer. Look to your patients."

"You are my patient," the healer pointed out drily. "If I give you one of my healing potions to improve your health, will you drink it, your Highness?"

Yi's back ached, as though he had become an old man while he slept. "If it will ease the pain in my back, yes."

He gulped down the bitter brew and handed the cup back to the healer. "Take care of our injured troops, healer. The Emperor may need them yet. For now Dean has fallen, the other northern cities may come seeking vengeance for our victory."

The healer's expression grew sombre. "Where will it end?"

"In a united empire, of course! Perhaps not in your lifetime or mine, but one day. For we are men, born to fight, and we always will." Yi grinned and strode out of the tent.

It wasn't until he was certain no one could see his face that he allowed himself to grimace at what he had to admit was a frightful pain in his back. It stung, like someone had stripped the skin from it. Yi had half a mind to strip the bandages from his torso and take a good look at the damage, but he was in too much of a hurry to bother with that now. Once he had spoken to General Li and was back in the privacy of his tent, then he could ask for Heng's help.

No, Heng should be in the capital, carrying his letter to the Emperor. The one about Mao's brilliance. Mao who had nearly died through General Li's bungled strategy. Ah, but it wasn't the General's strategy at all, but Mao's. No wonder the fool had made a mess of things. The Emperor needed more men like Mao, who were worth ten of General Li.

Yi swayed a little on his feet as he climbed the hill to the General's hut, but he put that down to not eating much since he'd left the city. Lack of food made a man weak. He would send for something directly, once he found the General.

The hut seemed unusually dark inside, but Yi stepped inside anyway, taking a moment to grab the doorframe as a strange bout of dizziness hit. "General Li!" he shouted.

"There he is now," General Li said. "The Emperor

is welcome to him."

Yi blinked. The General sat at his table, holding an open scroll in his hands. Heng looked haggard, but relieved. "Did you deliver my message to the Emperor?" Yi demanded.

Heng nodded. "He sent me back with his reply." He waved at Li's scroll.

Yi saw red. "First you try to get me killed, and now you're reading my personal letters from the Emperor? Have you no honour at all?" he roared.

General Li rose, his eyes flashing. "I am victorious. The city surrendered to me. Victory is mine, and you are to be sent home to the Emperor. Immediately."

Yi snorted. "The victory is Mao's, not yours. It was his strategy. And the Emperor knows it."

Li shrugged. "No one has seen the boy since he went into the city. An unfortunate casualty of war."

Yi's fury knew no bounds. "It wasn't me you tried to kill. It was Mao. A better man, and a better general than you will ever be. You failed, Uncle. Mao lives. And he will return to the capital with me, where I will tell my father every mistake and delay in this campaign has been your doing, and without Mao, we would still be sitting here, doing nothing!" Yi couldn't seem to catch his breath. The room was growing dark again and he couldn't stop it.

Yi swayed, unable to steady himself. Before Heng

could catch him, Yi toppled forward across the desk into oblivion.

Twenty-Three

Mai jerked awake, convinced her hands were afire. A quick glance told her this was not the case. In fact, her hands were bound in bandages and she was lying in a bed that also wasn't burning.

She shouldn't be in bed. Yi had been.

But the bed beside her was empty.

Mai jumped to her feet. "Where is he?" she demanded.

A healer she didn't recognise hurried toward her, making hushing sounds. "Where is who?"

Mai pointed a shaking figure at the empty bed. "Prince Yi, the Prince of Swords. He was injured in the battle."

"The Prince of Swords, lie in a soot-smeared bed, beside a boy so covered in ash and cinders you look like one of the kitchen drudges?" The healer laughed. "The prince would not be in a tent with the common soldiers. He will be in his own tent, or with the General. But the Prince of Swords cannot have been defeated. The news would be all over the camp by now if the Emperor's favourite son was injured, and all I have heard is about the General's victory over Dean. The city surrendered before the cooks rang the breakfast gong."

The battle had raged all night? How had she slept through it?

Realisation dawned. "What was in the tea I drank? Was it a sleeping draught?"

The healer shrugged. "I gave you nothing, so I do not know. But a sleeping patient is easier to treat than one who is awake, so we help many men to sleep."

"I shall not stay here a moment longer. I must find the prince," Mai said. Whatever the healer had heard, she knew otherwise. Yi was injured, and if he had tried to rejoin the battle in his condition…

She checked their tent first, but it was cold and deserted. No one had slept there last night. The practice ground was deserted, too, so she climbed the rise to the General's house.

In the doorway, she nearly bumped straight into the

healer she remembered from last night.

"You!" she exclaimed. "You drugged me, when you said you were giving me a pain draught. What did you do with Prince Yi?"

"It was a pain draught," the man said, drawing himself up. "It also relaxes a patient, so that many fall asleep. And the prince left my care, only to collapse in the General's arms. I have done what I can for him here, as he should not be moved." He glared at Mai as though she had suggested moving him.

"Will he be all right?" Mai demanded.

"He will live," the healer replied. "I shall return later, if the prince's condition changes. Until then, I have a hospital full of injured men to see to." He marched off down the hill.

Mai slipped inside. She found Yi in what looked like the General's own bedchamber, lying facedown on the bed. The General was nowhere to be seen.

"Yi, can you hear me?" she asked, her voice shaking more than she liked.

"What, did I finally manage to beat you, so you won't call me Rooster any more?" Yi turned his head and smiled weakly.

Mai breathed a sigh of relief. He could not be too badly hurt if he could make jokes. "The sun will rise in the west before you best me in a fight, Rooster. So much for watching each other's backs in the city. I had to carry you out on mine while you slept. What would the soldiers say if they knew their hero, the Prince of Swords, slept through the best part of the battle?"

"You carried me out?" Yi stared at her. "From what the healers tell me, I owe you my life. They say my armour caught fire, and if you hadn't stripped it off me, I would have burned, too. You are the hero of this battle, Mao, not me."

Mai didn't know what to say. She was no hero. She had not even fought in the battle. Much like Yi, she'd slept through it.

Yi continued, "And when we return to the capital, I will tell the Emperor so. He will give you a place at court, I am sure of it, and command you to marry, for great men like you should have sons to serve the Emperor when you go to join your ancestors." He winced. "The Emperor says I must travel to the capital immediately. But the healers tell me to wait, for I cannot ride like this. Not for a few days, at least. It feels like someone tried to flay me alive. I will be so scarred now, no woman will swoon over me. Even my bride will insist I bed her in the dark, so she doesn't have to see such scars."

"That's not true. You are still a prince, and I am certain every woman in the kingdom would be honoured to be chosen by a hero who is also the Emperor's favourite son." Bitterness welled up in Mai's belly as she said those words, for they incinerated whatever hopes she might have had, if only for a moment. But a prince – likely to be chosen as the Emperor's heir – was so far above her she would not even be allowed to sweep the floors in his bedchamber, let alone share his bed. Sharing his tent here was more than she deserved. Like the healer had said, once she returned home, she was destined to be no better than a kitchen drudge in her father's house, for if she never married, she would never be the mistress of any home at all. If only she never had to go home.

Yi grasped her hand. Despite the bandages, Mai felt his firm grip. "Promise me you will come to the capital, Mao," Yi said. "So that if I must do as the Emperor commands and choose a bride, I will have your sage advice to guide me and lift my spirits should things go wrong. I can face an enemy army with no fear, but an army of women? I will need a hero like you by my side to bolster my courage."

Mai laughed. "A rooster who runs away from a flock of hens? I wouldn't miss such a sight for all the riches in the world. I will come to the capital with you."

And watch him choose a bride, while her heart died a little inside. She had come to Dean to fight in a war. The war was won, but Mai feared she might have lost something far more important – her heart, hopelessly in love with Prince Yi.

Twenty-Four

"The Prince of Swords will not ride home in a litter," Yi grumbled when he saw the conveyance. "They are for invalids and ladies, not warriors."

Mai privately agreed, but it would not do to tell him so. "Officially, your great friend Yeong Mao, who was grievously wounded in the battle, will ride in the litter. The Prince of Swords will ride alongside it as his honour guard, and occasionally within to share his wit and wisdom with the poor invalid."

Yi dropped his voice so low only Mai could hear it. "I still cannot ride. In another few days, perhaps…"

A few days would turn into a week, and Mai knew it would be many weeks before Yi fully recovered. She had seen his bloodied back when Heng and the healers had changed his bandages that very morning. The Emperor demanded his son return home, and the Emperor must be obeyed. Especially when the General wanted Mai dead for daring to win the war, and had begun to look at Yi in the same way. Mai had found the perfect solution to prevent them both from being assassinated.

Mai sighed. "Heng will dress me in your armour, and I will ride like a rooster for as long as I need to, puffing and preening until all the men know it is you who is astride that horse. Then, when we are far enough away from camp, I will join you in the litter and do my best to stop you from getting bored."

Yi managed a faint smile. "We could take some dancing girls and musicians."

Mai felt a pang of homesickness as she remembered her sisters practicing dancing and music day and night, determined to perform well enough to catch the eye of a prince.

"And ruin the illusion? It is less than two days' journey to the capital – you said so yourself. If you truly grow bored, I will…recite poetry for you." Mai managed a wicked grin. "One of the boys on the watchtower near the gate has penned quite a pretty one. He sent you a copy to take with you to the Emperor."

Mai watched Yi try to hide how much he hated poetry. "Must I hear it?"

"If the Emperor loves poetry as much as you say, I am sure it will be quite the favourite at court. It describes how you and the General rode side by side, leading the charge into the city, as everyone bowed low before you."

"He's too much of a coward to do any such thing," Yi declared. "Are you sure we can't have some musicians?"

Mai sighed. "Only if you want them to sing about how the Prince of Swords had to be carried home by litter after the battle, instead of riding proudly on his horse."

Yi managed a wry smile. "I think you care about my honour even more than I do, Mao. One day, when my head is not so befuddled with healing potions, remind me to thank you."

Between Heng and Mai, Yi drank enough healing potions to keep him sleeping soundly for most of the journey back to the capital, to Mai's considerable relief. No musicians needed.

As they approached the palace, Mai grew quiet, glad Yi's helmet hid her face and, more importantly, her gaping mouth. If a giant had taken her father's house, all the houses in the village, and every other noble's house in the kingdom, and piled them up harmoniously into one enormous structure, it still wouldn't convey the sheer magnitude of the Emperor's palace. It made even the city of Dean look tiny.

More than ever, Mai truly believed she did not belong here at court. Her stepmother had been right.

If it weren't for Yi, she would have left the moment he was safely home, but as he was lifted from the litter, he seized her arm and refused to let go. "You must stay with me in my apartments. My uncle has spies in court who might yet try to kill you. You will be safe with me."

Privately, Mai thought she would be safer without Yi, for she was more than a match for him, and if he was the best swordsman in the kingdom…no one else would even get close. Safer than even Yi believed. So she followed her heart and the prince inside the maze that was the imperial palace.

Twenty-Five

Though impatience ate at him, Yi waited until Heng had installed Mao in the spacious sleeping chamber beside his own before he shared his joke.

"Do you like your room?" Yi asked.

Mao nodded and thanked him.

"Just don't take any clothes from the chests in there. It belongs to my mistress," Yi told him with a grin.

Mao's jaw dropped. "Where will your mistress sleep while I am here?"

Yi was laughing too hard to answer, so Heng did it for him. "The prince has no mistress. Anything in that room belonged to the mistress of the man who had this apartment before the prince. The Emperor has many guest apartments where you might have slept, but the prince insists you stay here, in a room which cannot be reached without crossing his chambers first."

Mao nodded as if he understood. "So I am to be kept hidden here?" he asked.

"Of course not. You are free to move about the palace as you wish, as my guest," Yi said. "But a man must sleep."

"And what do I tell anyone who asks who I am?" Mao asked. "I can hardly say I am your mistress."

Both Yi and Heng laughed at that. Mao might not be a large man, but he was no beauty. Nor did he have the respectful demeanour of one of the court women. Mao might mock Yi's pride, but his was no less, Yi knew. And why not? Mao had much to be proud of.

"Tell them the truth. That you are Yeong Mao, the hero of the siege of Dean, and the Prince of Swords' closest friend." Yi smiled at Mao's blush. He was no longer a boy, but a man, yet he still blushed like a maiden.

"If I tell them the whole truth, that I am the friend of a rooster who I beat daily in every bout we fight, no one will believe me," Mao said.

"That is because all court men are roosters by your reckoning, and they won't know which one you mean,"

Yi replied. He wanted to laugh, but he knew all too well how true it was. "Keep your sword on you at all times, and be on your guard. They will be no match for you. After all, I, the best swordsman there is, am no match for you."

Mao smiled sadly, as though he wished things were different.

One day, Yi promised himself. When he was healed and could seek out Mao's father to train him. Then they would meet on the training ground as equals, and Mao would truly test his skill.

One day soon.

Sighing, he led the way.

Twenty-Six

Mai need not have worried. In her ordinary clothing, no one paid her much notice at all. Meals were served in the prince's quarters, and at those times she joined him, but the rest of the day was her own to do with as she wished. At first, she explored the palace, but she was terrified of wandering into the court or some place a minor country noble did not belong. For all Yi's talk of her being a hero, she didn't feel like much at all.

What she wanted most was a chance to rebalance herself, to train in the martial dances her father had taught her, but she wasn't sure which of the many courtyards and gardens in the palace would be appropriate.

Finally, she asked Heng, who directed her to the training yard Yi usually used. When she stepped into the battleground of straw practice dummies and targets, she understood why he fought as he did. Yi had never truly trained against a worthy opponent here. Neither would she, but she did not need to. Simply performing the exercises would be enough for now.

She moved through the martial dance with her eyes closed, imagining herself home with her father. Oh, but she missed him, and her sisters. She even missed Jing, for all her complaints and commands, for they were her family. They were home. And she was…here, a tiny, insignificant bug who did not belong in the behemoth that was the imperial palace.

But she did not belong at home, either. Her father had Jing to take care of him. If she returned, he would only try to find her some sort of husband. A man who wouldn't care about the size of her feet. But she could never love him, for Yi already held her heart, and he would never know, for Mai could never tell him.

Mai kicked out at a practice dummy, and was gratified to see its head fall off and roll away. She trotted across the sand to retrieve the head, but what she found diminished her pride considerably. The straw that filled the sacking head was so old and rotten it had nearly disintegrated. A puff of wind might have carried it away, if Mai's foot had not done so.

This was Yi's favourite place to train, she reminded herself. No one had used any of this since he went to war. He would not thank her for destroying the place.

Now she felt less balanced than ever. So much for training helping her.

With a sigh of resignation, Mai returned to the prince's apartments. The chime of the palace's water clock – a wonder that took some getting used to – signalled the quarter hour. She must have been too engrossed in her training to miss the full complement of gongs and bells and the general cacophony that occurred to mark the hour. Or perhaps it was not audible in the prince's training yard – yet another reason to spend more time there.

She heard the low murmur of voices as she entered Yi's apartments, coming from his bedchamber. Not wanting to interrupt, she edged toward her own rooms to wash and change into fresh clothes for the day. She might look like a man, but she had no intention of smelling like one.

A long time passed, but Yi did not call her name. Curiosity got the better of her, so she left her room to try to discover who his visitor was.

"He is a fiercer warrior than you. I can see why you like his company," a male voice said. "In the practice yard just now, I saw him decapitating a practice dummy like you used to do. Only he didn't use a sword."

Mai's face grew hot. Yi's visitor had been watching her train?

"He would make a good captain of your personal guard when you are Emperor," the man continued. "The way he moves…he has the grace of the most skilled dancers, hypnotising you, even as he delivers a killing blow. I have never seen anything like it. And yet you tell me he devised the strategy that ended the siege, when no one believed such a thing was even possible? A strategist and a fighter. A rare combination, making him a very dangerous man. Are you sure of his loyalty?"

"He saved my life, Father," Yi said. "Carried my unconscious body through a battlefield to camp. If that is not loyalty, I don't know what is."

Realisation felled her with a flurry of blows. Yi was talking to the Emperor about her in the next room. The Emperor who had watched her train and now considered her dangerous. Questioned her loyalty. As though she would do anything to endanger the Emperor, or the man she loved.

"For that alone, I would do as you ask, but what of the man? I have never heard of him before your letters about him, and you speak of nothing else but this man. You sound like a man in love."

Yi liked men? Was that why he hadn't yet married? Mai's eyes widened. Yet she'd shared a tent with him every night, spent so much time with him, and not once had she seen so much as a spark of lust in his eyes. Of course, there was that one night after the skirmish in one of the blockade camps, when the camp followers had tried to tempt them both into a tryst. Lust had certainly burned in Yi's eyes then, but not when he looked at her. No, his eyes had been on the woman, riding her soldier lover hard into their battle for shared pleasure. Or so it had seemed at the time.

"A superior sparring partner is easier to find than a willing bride, Father. I wager you have a hundred willing women lined up for me when I am well, but I have searched all my adult life for a man who could cross swords with me and win. I am no longer the Prince of Swords, for Mao conquers me every time we step onto the training ground." Yi laughed. "I protected your poets, giving them guard duty where they would be far from harm. All I ask in return is that you honour one man. A man who deserves your attention because of his deeds, not because of the words he might one day write."

"When you are fully healed, you may introduce him to me. See that you obey the healers and stay abed until then, boy, for I need you well. Well enough to attend the ball, choose a bride, and beget sons with her!"

"Yes, Father." Yi sounded unusually meek.

A man in purple robes swept out of the apartment, not sparing a glance for where Mai crouched behind a stone statue, for which she was grateful.

Heng, carrying the breakfast tray, was more observant. "I have the lychees you like, Mao, and peaches for the prince. The cook tells me there will be apricots tomorrow, if you wish."

Mai longed for apricots, picked fresh from her father's orchard. "Yes, please."

"I begin to think Heng likes you more than he does me," Yi called from his room. "How much did you hear?"

Mai saw no point in lying. "I did not see him watching me at training," she admitted as she pulled up a chair.

"When he was younger, my father did not know he would be Emperor. He was a younger son, and not even one of his father's favourites. He learned stealth as a way to survive at court, which served him well when a palace coup killed his father and many of his brothers. He alone survived, to become the Emperor we all know and love," Yi said.

Mai chose not to contradict him. All she knew of the Emperor was that he loved his son, cared for his health and wished him to have sons of his own.

"He is still set on finding me a bride, but he also wants to meet you. The healers have told us in three weeks I will be well enough to leave my bed. So, in four weeks, my father will throw a ball. He has invited every noble girl eligible to be my bride, and I must choose one of them." His eyes held pain as he turned his gaze on Mai. "What if I choose wrong?"

"You won't," Mai soothed. "Listen to your heart, and follow where it leads. Think of what you want most in a bride, and watch for it. You are a prince. What woman would refuse you?"

"I don't want a woman afraid to refuse me, or one who only wishes to marry a prince!" Yi declared, slamming his hand down on the table, making the peach slices jump. "I want a woman like the ones the poets sing songs about. Their loyalty, their courage…oh, pretty, too, I supposed, and graceful. What are your sisters like?"

Mai blinked, not sure she'd heard the question correctly. "My…my sisters?"

"Yes. What are they like?"

Mai wet her lips. "Much like any other girls, I guess. At the age I started to learn the martial dance my father taught me, they began to learn court dances. With so much practice, they can't help but be good dancers." Not that she knew, because she hadn't been able to bear to watch them wince as their bound feet hurt. "They're very sweet. They deserve to marry well, to men who will care for them for the rest of their lives. Isn't that the most a girl can hope for?"

Yi opened his mouth to respond, then closed it again, as though he'd decided not to air his true answer. Finally, he said, "Perhaps."

A hope that was beyond Mai now, she knew, but at least her friend could be happy in his choice of wife. "I saw your training yard this morning. Now I know why you are such a terrible fighter. Did your weapons master never tell you that straw men cannot fight back?"

Yi laughed, and breakfast became a merry affair where the Emperor's visit was soon forgotten.

Twenty-Seven

Every day she spent in the palace, the wider Mai felt the chasm grew between palace life and hers. Here, there were hordes of servants ready to obey her every whim, but at home, she would have served Jing instead. And yet...every day she spent in Yi's company she fell deeper in love with the man.

She longed to tell him the truth, but the illusion that had allowed her to meet him in the first place was now a curse that kept her true identity a secret from the man she wished to hide nothing from. Especially when it became clear that he would be forced to choose a bride at the Emperor's ball. She knew there was little chance of him choosing her over the delicate, beautiful creatures arriving at court every day, but until he rejected her, her silly heart still held out hope that she might be the woman he chose. But as long as the illusion made her look like a man, Yi would never believe she was a woman at all.

She spent an extra hour training every morning, and another at sunset, working off her frustrations until Yi's straw dummies had no stuffing left to lose. It was never enough. Was she to remain a man for the rest of her life?

A man who could not find a bride, for she lacked the necessary parts to make a marriage fruitful, something any bride she tried to take would surely notice.

Sighing, she gave up for the day, returning to the prince's apartments by the light of the newly lit torches, for it was well past sunset now. Yi had been allowed out of bed briefly in order to be measured for splendid new clothes, but the Emperor had stationed guards outside his door to make sure he did not leave his apartment. No one stopped Mai from entering, though.

She found a lost-looking serving girl who appeared vaguely familiar standing in the middle of Yi's receiving room. The prince himself was nowhere in sight, so she addressed the girl: "What are you doing in these private chambers?"

The girl held out a basket. "I brought a gift, your Highness. The sweetest mountain apricots you have ever tasted, as a gift from Yeong Fu in thanks for his invitation to the ball."

"Yeong Fu is at court?" Mai blurted out.

"No, your Highness, but his family has come for the ball." She shoved the basket under Mai's nose. "Take one and taste it, your Highness."

One apricot stood out, bigger and more perfect than the others. Why, it almost seemed to glow. That couldn't be right. Mai had never seen an apricot glow before.

"What magic is this?" she demanded. She would not let Jing cast a spell on the prince.

The girl's eyes dropped to her shoes. "No magic at all, your Highness. Just the rich soil, water from icy mountain streams and clean air makes fruit such as this."

"Not one I've ever seen before," Mai said grimly, reaching for the offending fruit. "I don't know what your mistress is playing at, but it stops now." Her fingers closed around the apricot, which seemed to hum happily in her hand. Definitely not normal. "Take me to your mistress, so that I can tell her myself."

The girl's horrified eyes met Mai's, before she ducked her head again. "Yes, your Highness," she said.

Mai considered telling the girl she wasn't the prince,

but decided against it. She would find out the truth soon enough.

Jing's voice rang out the moment the maid walked into the guest apartment: "And? Did the prince eat his apricot?"

"No, madam. He…he…" The girl waved wordlessly at Mai.

Jing slapped the girl across her face. "Stupid country bumpkin. I knew I should have sent someone else. That is not the prince. He's just some common soldier."

Mai drew herself up. "I am no common soldier. I am Yeong Mai, the hero of the siege of Dean, stepmother. Do you not recognise the illusion you cast?" Slowly, she spun on the spot.

Jing's mouth hung open in shock. "Mai? You are still alive? You have been away from home so long. I thought you'd surely been killed, or worse. What are you doing here?"

Mai tossed the apricot into the air and caught it. "Saving the prince from your spells, it would seem."

Jing shrugged. "It is just a little help, is all. It's not like he needs the encouragement. The prince himself requested that we come to the ball. The Emperor's letter arrived weeks ago, commanding us to come to the palace." She brandished a scroll that held pride of place on the table. "See? The prince demands the daughters of Yeong Fu to present themselves at the palace, so that he might choose one of them for his bride."

Now it was Mai's turn to have trouble closing her mouth. "Lin and Lei? They are but children. Not old enough to be betrothed, let alone married to Prince Yi!"

Jing's smile was smug. "You have been away a long time. My girls have grown up." Footsteps sounded in the corridor outside. "And here they are, back from court."

The girls who minced in looked like Lin and Lei, but stretched, somehow. Thinner and taller, yet painted to look like porcelain dolls. Mai did the sums in her head, before the abacus beads clicked into place properly. She shook her head.

"They are only thirteen. You have worked some magic on them, just as you have done on me. You have turned them into grown women when they are still children!" Mai wanted to be sick at the thought of Yi taking one of these girls to bed on his wedding night. She would not let that happen. Not to him, and not to them.

"Keep your voice down!" Jing ordered. "If anyone finds a strange man in the girls' chamber, you will ruin their chances with the prince. They have been working toward this their whole lives. Perhaps they are a little young, but a young bride is a biddable one, and they have so many more fertile years ahead of them. Lin or Lei would both be perfect brides for the prince, and if I must make them a little older…why, the other court women think nothing of painting and padding their daughters. I simply made the illusion more believable."

"No." Mai shook her head. "I will not let you trick the prince into this. You must break the spell on me. Let me go in their stead. If the prince demands a daughter of Yeong Fu, I will go to the ball."

For the first time, Mai's heart soared. If she attended the ball, she would make certain Yi noticed her. Then she would have her answer, and have no need to tell him of her subterfuge in order to join the army. Why, he need never know she was Mao at all.

"You?" Jing scoffed. "A girl with the iron lotus feet of a peasant, enter the court so that she might catch the eye of the prince? I don't think so. You haven't a chance of catching a husband, let alone a prince, and you will only ruin the girls' chances if anyone learns you are associated with them. No. You shall not go to the ball."

Her heart sank, right into her mother's shoes. What was Mai thinking? Even if she went, Yi would never choose her over the hundreds of more eligible maidens.

"Perhaps if you made my feet appear as small as

yours," Mai began eagerly.

"I will not!" Jing interrupted. "You cannot dance, or do any of the things expected of a court lady. The only thing you know how to hold is a sword. Go back to the army where you belong. You will never marry, and you will not go to a ball in the imperial court, where you have no place!"

Tears sprang to Mai's eyes. Tears the hero of the siege of Dean could not cry where anyone would see him. Tears Jing did not deserve to see, either.

So Mai did the only thing she could think of – she fled to the training yard from whence she'd come.

Twenty Eight

The yard was dark, for no torches were lit there at night. Mai stumbled through the gardens, swearing as she struggled to find the path again. Had she somehow entered the wrong courtyard instead? She didn't remember there being quite so many bushes before.

She tripped over a rock, barking her shin on the way down. Instinct told her to roll, to recover, so that she might regain her feet and fight on, but Mai resisted. She barely felt the impact as she hit the ground. She had fought too long for too much that she could never have. Prince Yi would never be hers, and she could not bear to go to a ball to watch him choose someone else.

Lying facedown on the gravel path, she started to sob in earnest. What did it matter? No one would see her here.

She should have known better. Nothing in the palace went unobserved. There were spies everywhere.

A small, feminine cough sounded from Mai's left.

Maybe if Mai ignored her, she would go away.

"Why are you crying?" a voice asked, dashing Mai's hopes.

"I am not crying," Mai snapped. "I have simply fallen and when I landed, dust irritated my eyes."

"I see no dust, Mai," the woman said, stepping forward so Mai could see her. Though there were no torches, the woman was clearly visible, as though she emitted a glow of her own. Her purple gown marked her as one of the Emperor's family, though her eyes were rounder than any Mai had seen before. And purple, the same shade as her gown, which was made in a fashion unlike any Mai had seen women wear in the palace.

If the Emperor could spy on her unseen, then this woman could only be one person.

"I am sorry, your Majesty," Mai said. "I would bow, but I am already prostrate. What dust there was has settled in my eyes."

The woman laughed. "I am no queen. No throne is worth sharing a bed with a king." She gave a delicate shudder. "I am Zuleika. Merely a lady, though not of this court, or any other."

"Are you here for the prince, too?" Mai asked. Yi would like this one, she was sure of it. Lady Zuleika had all the bearing of an empress who would bow before no one.

"In a small way, yes, but I have no wish to meet the man. I came here because of your shoes," Zuleika said.

Mai sat up, wincing. Perhaps she should have landed better. "My shoes?"

"Well, truthfully, because of my mother, and your mother's shoes," Zuleika went on. She laughed again. "You'd think I'd be better at this, given who my mother was and all, but in my defence, this is my first time."

"Your first time for what?" Now Mai was really confused. The Lady Zuleika had known her mother? She looked barely older than Mai herself.

"Why, being a proper fairy godmother, of course!"

Mai stared. "A fairy…what?"

Zuleika sighed. "Did your mother ever tell you how she came to own those shoes?"

"They were a gift," Mai began haltingly. "She was a girl in her father's camp, and the camp followers would steal her shoes and hide them, for her father had forbidden her from leaving his tent unless she was properly dressed, and she could not leave without shoes. She wished to meet with one of the young officers, the man who would later become my father, and dance for him at the victory celebration, but the other girls were jealous, and – "

"And my mother came upon her, crying, alone, much like you are now, and listened to her troubles. She gave her this pair of shoes, promising that they would grant her balance and grace for the dance of her life, and that they would never be lost," Zuleika finished with a smile. "And so your mother married your father, and they won many victories together, until they retired from war and had you."

Mai still didn't understand. "So your mother was my mother's fairy godmother, but it still does not explain to me why you are here."

Zuleika grinned. "A prince choosing a bride among hundreds of maidens from throughout the land? It sounds like a fairy tale come true. Why wouldn't a fairy godmother want to go to a ball such as this? Why wouldn't any maiden want to go?" She nodded at Mai. "Well, don't you?"

Mai found herself nodding. "Of course, but…I have nothing to wear, and my stepmother is right that no prince will want a girl who looks like a commoner when he could choose ladies raised for court life. I have no place there."

Zuleika made a derisive noise in her throat. "Your

place is at the prince's side. You know it. He knows it. Even your shoes know it."

Mai laughed. "Shoes do not think."

Zuleika winked. "Don't underestimate the power in a magical object, and you have two with you always. If you wear those shoes to the ball, I promise the prince will not leave your side. He will dance only with you, and at the end of the night, no illusion will hide what you truly are from him."

"But my stepmother – "

"Is a witch of little talent, who can only cast illusions. They look and feel real enough, but she is no enchantress. Not like I am." Zuleika held out her hand. "Mai, on the night of the ball, I shall wait here until that unbelievably noisy clock contraption strikes midnight. If you wish to have the illusion removed so that the prince can see you as you truly are, you must come to me here and I will undo Jing's spell. Or I can turn the prince into a frog, if you prefer. Not all of them are as charming as they first appear, though I'm sure your prince is the perfect gentleman. In the meantime…how about we do a little something about those shoes?"

Mai glanced down at the worn red silk. "They are the only thing I have left of my mother's," she whispered.

"But she would not mind if I made them pretty

enough for court, and perhaps wove a little of my own magic into them, too?" Zuleika asked.

Mai managed a smile. "I'm sure she wouldn't mind."

Zuleika bit her lip. "How forgetful are you? Because what I have in mind would mean removing that never-lose-your-shoes spell."

"I have never lost my shoes, not forgotten them," Mai assured her.

Zuleika clapped her hands. "Good. Then I know just what to do."

Twenty-Nine

Still puzzled by her encounter with the strange Lady Zuleika, who dressed like a foreign empress yet claimed to be her fairy godmother, Mai headed back to Yi's apartments. She took longer than usual, because she kept stopping to admire her shoes, which caught the light in the most amazing ways. Zuleika had turned the faded red silk into something that shimmered partway between blue and green before covering the silk in a myriad of glass beads, which caught the light and threw it in all directions. They were ornamental shoes for court, never to be worn on a battlefield again.

Mai laughed quietly to herself. If she ever set foot

on a battlefield wearing these, she would dazzle the enemy without having to unsheathe her sword.

Lady Zuleika had known her name, and seen through Jing's illusion.

The realisation stopped her dead. Perhaps the woman truly was her fairy godmother, despite her youth. But she had said her mother was Da Ying's fairy godmother, so perhaps these things were passed down from mother to daughter. Had Zuleika inherited her mother's responsibilities? If she had, that mean that her mother walked the spirit world now, just like Da Ying.

More confident in Zuleika's predictions now, Mai couldn't keep the smile off her face as she walked into Yi's sitting room.

"So you have already heard," Yi greeted her. "Who told you? Was it Heng?"

Mai stumbled to a halt. "Heard what? I was training, and then I saw my sisters, and I have only just arrived back here. I have not seen Heng since this morning."

"Good," Yi beamed. "Your sisters are here, and so are your court clothes. My new ones, too, but they are of little consequence – just something to wear to the ball. My mother said you would need court clothes, so Heng took care of it. What do you think?"

Mai surveyed the piles of neatly folded blue silk that

seemed to cover every surface. "Do men really wear such bright colours at court?" she asked carefully. She already knew the ladies dressed so brightly they looked like exotic butterflies, but most of the noblemen she'd seen wore robes in dark shades of purple, red, black and green. Not until today had she seen men's clothing in this azure blue that reminded her of the mountain lakes at home on a sunny day. Or the colour of her shoes.

Yi laughed. "Men are much like peacocks in court. You have spent weeks in the palace, yet you have never attended court. Once the ball is over, that will change. I will introduce you to the Emperor, and you will spend as much time in court as you desire. Let's hope for another war before your enthusiasm wanes."

War. Would that be her life now, if Jing would not allow her to go home? It would be a lonely life, but at least it was an honourable one. "Perhaps," Mai agreed.

"This is what you will wear to the ball," Yi said eagerly, pointing at a particularly bright robe the exact same shade as Mai's shoes. "As the crown prince, I must wear a hideous shade of yellow that makes me look like an apricot." He gestured at his own gold silk robes, which were much more richly embroidered than Mai's.

Mai laid the two robes side by side. "You will be the sun, blinding everyone, while I stand at your shoulder, the azure sky in the background."

"I would rather be back at the siege of Dean than walk into that ballroom tomorrow night to select my bride," Yi admitted. "But if you are there, all eyes will be on you as the war hero. I daresay more girls will look to you as a suitable husband than me. We will choose brides together, you and I."

There was only one way they could both choose their life partners together, and even though Mai's fairy godmother had foretold it, she still didn't believe it was possible. "I will take no bride, but I will help you choose yours. I hope you choose a girl who will make you happy all your days."

"I'll settle for one who does not make me rue my decision before the week is out," Yi said, so low Mai didn't think she was supposed to hear it.

She fervently hoped he would get his wish.

Thirty

The peacock dance. Why did they always have to perform the peacock dance? It was true what his old teacher said about all colours being blinding, Yi realised now. With so much brightness, the dancing women became a blur. How could a man choose one bride when they all looked the same?

He spared a glance for Mao, who seemed too intent on the contents of his cup to care about the dancers, either. But then, Mao had never cared much for music and dancing girls.

"Which girl do you think is the most beautiful?" Yi asked, nudging him.

Mao took a long time before he answered, "I would

have to say my sisters. I haven't seen them in so long, that they would hold my attention even if they were dressed in rags."

Yi's curiosity burned to see the sisters he had not yet met. "Where are they?"

Mao pointed at two girls who wore layered robes in shades of purple and gold. The Emperor's colours, which no other girls had dared to wear.

Yi stared at them hungrily. One of them held the key to his happiness, he was sure of it, but even as he focussed on one and then the other, he felt nothing. Oh, they were graceful enough dancers, and as pretty as any of the other dancing dolls, but Yi had felt more while watching camp followers capering around the campfire with common soldiers at one of the victory celebrations. He didn't understand why these girls should leave him so unmoved.

"Which do you think would make a better bride?" he asked.

Mao laughed uncertainly. "I could not answer that. Lin and Lei are my sisters. The last time I saw them, they were children, and even now they are only twelve or thirteen years old. Too young to be brides, if you ask me."

"My father has decreed that girls can marry as young as fourteen now," Yi said.

Mao frowned. "Just because they can, doesn't mean

they should. Do you want a bride who is still a child, or a woman grown? You said you wanted a woman of loyalty and courage, who does not fear you. If you bed a child and hurt her, she will fear you all her days."

As always, Mao was right. He didn't want one of Da Ying's daughters to fear him. Who knew what she might do if she regarded her husband as her enemy?

An idea began to grow in the back of his mind. His father had insisted he choose a bride tonight, but he'd never said he needed to marry the girl immediately. It would give him the perfect excuse to meet with Yeong Fu in the morning to discuss a betrothal for a marriage some time in the future…and in the meantime, he would be a willing pupil to his future father-in-law.

"Doesn't watching all this make you want to dance?" Yi asked Mao.

Mao shook his head. "I only know one dance, Rooster, and it is a martial one. This is hardly the place."

Yi grinned. "I know just the place, and I will show you. I shall speak to my father for a moment, and then we will be free."

He took a moment to compose himself before he approached his father.

"Excuse me, your Majesty," Yi said, bowing. "I have made my decision."

His father's eyebrows rose. "I hope it is a wise one."

Yi prayed that it would be.

Thirty-One

Yi kept his voice low so that only those closest to him would hear. That included the Emperor, the Empress and Mai herself, for there was not even a servant within earshot, Mai noticed with relief.

"I wish to take Yeong Fu's daughter as my bride," Yi said.

Mao smothered a gasp. After all she had said, he still wanted one of the girls?

"Which one? I understand he has several," the Emperor said.

"I'm not certain," Yi admitted. "But they are too young yet, so I will negotiate the betrothal with Fu, and make my decision then. When I have his agreement, then we can set a wedding date."

Mai breathed again. So he had not made a decision after all. And when Yi spoke to her father, he would suggest Yi marry his oldest daughter, and not Lin or Lei. Perhaps she still stood a chance with the prince, however slim.

"Very well," the Emperor said.

Mai felt the uncanny sensation that someone was staring at her. She glanced around, only to meet the eyes of the Empress herself. Flustered, Mai bowed deeply. She had heard that General Li was the Empress' brother, which surely meant the woman wanted her dead as much as the General did.

"Come, we are free," Yi said, grabbing Mai's arm.

Willingly, she let herself be led out of the ballroom and into a corridor full of surprised servants. Amid a flurry of bowing, Yi dragged her through the throng to a courtyard where all was still and dark.

Yi was having none of it, though. He seized a torch and used it to light several more, before thrusting the first into the sand that marked a sparring ring surrounded by garden. This was not his usual practice yard, but another part of the palace entirely.

Yi fanned out the hem of his robe like a tail and lifted his hand in imitation of a peacock head, much like the girls in the ballroom had done. "Will you dance with me, Mao?" He nodded at the wooden practice swords stuck point first into the sand at the end of the ring.

"A rooster in the field, and a peacock at court. Are you sure you are recovered enough to dance, Rooster?" Mai asked, smiling to ease the sting of her words.

Yi snatched up one of the swords, swinging it experimentally. "We shall see, but you don't know how much I've missed dancing with you. The mornings when it was just you and me, against a whole army. No one else at court understands. Only you."

Mai selected a wooden sword, testing its balance. It would do. "You have missed the mouthfuls of sand I made you eat, every time you fell on your face in the ring? Perhaps your illness has addled your wits. The last time we sparred, I distinctly recall you cursing my ancestors for begetting children with barbarian war gods." She lifted the blade in a relaxed fighting pose.

"I really said that?" Yi's gaze sank from Mai's face to her feet. "You're going to fight me in your court shoes? Those?"

In the light of the torch, her shoes seemed to glow gold, reflecting the flames in all directions. Mai's mother's shoes had never looked so splendid.

She shrugged. "I will still beat you, no matter what I wear. Court robes or armour, army boots or my mother's shoes. But if you think they will distract you,

I shall remove them." Mai slipped off her shoes and set them on the grass beside the ring.

"Court clothes are hardly good for dancing," Yi said, stripping off his outer robes so he stood in only his trousers.

Mai's mouth suddenly grew dry. The way the firelight seemed to glow as it caressed the muscles of his chest…her hands itched to trace each of them in turn, from his taut belly up to his shoulders, before cupping his face for a kiss.

Where had that thought come from? she wondered, muttering something about following suit as she shrugged out of her blue outer robe. She kept the rest of her clothes, though, not wanting to be nearly naked with him here, where anyone could see them. By the ancestors, she still looked like a man!

"Tell me when you tire," she said. "You are out of practice, after all."

They crossed swords lightly, focussing on their footwork more than the clash of blades. They danced in a circle, never taking their eyes from one another, as the balance seemed to flow from one to the other as never before. For all that he was out of practice, Yi had learned much in their time together.

Mai darted in, tapping his shoulder with her blade, and Yi laughed.

"By the ancestors, that feels good," he said.

It was Mai's turn to laugh. "You will not say that in the morning, when your bruises start to show."

"Yes, I will!" he declared. "For in the morning, we shall dance again. I have lain abed long enough!"

She smiled. "If you wish." If she had her way, the illusion that made her a man would be gone by morning. What would Yi say to sparring with her then?

The chiming water clock bells began to ring, signifying the changing of the hour. "What time is it?" Mai asked.

Yi cocked his head to one side, listening. "Midnight, I think. Yes, that's twelve."

The sword fell from Mai's suddenly nerveless fingers. "Midnight already? No! I have to meet…I must…" Without even pausing to finish her sentence, she took to her heels, running through the corridors until she reached the practice yard where she'd first met her fairy godmother.

"Lady Zuleika?" she called, then repeated it, louder still.

No response.

"Lady Zuleika!"

No matter how many times Mai said the woman's name, she did not appear.

Mai would be forced to remain a man forever, as she watched the man she loved marry one of her sisters.

Mai fell to her knees and burst into tears.

Thirty-Two

So Mao had a midnight tryst? The sly fox. All that talk of never taking a bride and he'd arranged to meet some girl in the middle of the night. Laughing quietly to himself, Yi sat down on a bench to wait. If Mao wasn't back soon, he'd head off to bed. Prince or not, he still wanted to look well-rested when he asked Mao's father for one of his daughters' hands on the morrow.

When he started to feel the chill of the night air, he pulled on his court clothes again. When he picked up the gaudy gold robe, he was surprised to see Mao's shoes underneath. He'd been in such a hurry, he'd left without his shoes. Yi picked them up and set them on the bench beside him. For shoes, they were quite remarkable, catching whatever light there was and holding tight to it in the strangely angular glass beads sewn all over them. Any woman in court would gladly give her eyeteeth to own shoes that sparkled like the sun in the light of a torch – and yet they belonged to Mao. He'd never seen them before, Yi was certain – if he had, he would have remembered. And they were so small, too. Yi could not fit his foot inside one of the shoes. He knew Mao was smaller than him, but he'd never thought he had small feet before. If Yi didn't know better, he would have sworn he held a pair of women's shoes.

Heng would know. He must have commissioned these for Mao along with the rest of his court clothes.

Deciding that Mao was probably too busy with his girl friend to return any time soon, Yi rose and made his way back to his apartment, carrying Mao's shoes. He set them on the table in the sitting room, then proceeded to remove his uncomfortable court clothes.

"Those are pretty," Heng said when he walked in. "Are they a gift for your new bride?"

Yi frowned. "No. They're Mao's. Don't you recognise them? He wore them to the ball tonight."

Heng circled the table, admiring them from every angle. "They can't be his. Those are much too small." He lifted a pair of brand-new silk shoes on the table, made in the same style as the ones Yi had just kicked off. "These are the shoes Mao was supposed to wear tonight. See? Much larger."

Yi shook his head. "But he was wearing these. I saw him wearing them, then take them off, with my own eyes." He waved at Heng. "Find me another pair of his shoes from his sleeping cubicle."

Heng nodded and did as he was bid, but he came back a few minutes later, empty handed. "There aren't any. I've only ever seen him wear one pair of shoes, and they're not there."

Mao would explain things on his return, Yi was certain. He wasn't a man to keep secrets. Perhaps the shoes Heng had commissioned were too big, and he'd been forced to take whatever the tailor had spare. That something like this would be spare, though…

Yi found the jug of baijiu he and Mao had been drinking before the ball, and poured himself a cup. The strong spirit seared his throat on the way down, a potent reminder not to drink too much of the stuff. He settled down to wait for Mao.

He was woken from a doze by quiet footsteps. A girl wearing the colourless clothing of a drudge entered the room, glanced about, then headed for the table where Mao's shoes lay. Without hesitation, she snatched them up.

"Put those down!" Yi roared, leaping to his feet.

"Get out!"

Startled, the girl stared at him for a moment before she remembered herself and bowed. "I must…"

"Do you know who I am?" he demanded.

Without raising her eyes to his face, the girl nodded.

"Who am I?"

"His Highness, the Prince of Swords," she whispered.

"And you would dare to steal from me?" he thundered.

"I wasn't – " she began.

"Not another word, or I shall call the palace guards and have you thrown out. Tell whatever woman who sent you that I have chosen my bride and no trick or spell will change my mind. Now get out!"

The girl hesitated for a moment, then she bowed even lower than before and scurried out.

Yi checked Mao's room, but the man had not yet returned. Perhaps he was spending the night with his mistress. A sly dog indeed. Shaking his head, Yi headed to his bed. Answers could wait until morning.

Thirty-Three

Her fairy godmother wasn't the only one who could remove the illusion. Jing could, too, Mai realised, wiping her eyes. The ball was finished and Yi had made his decision. Jing had won. Which meant Mai had nothing left to lose if she demanded her stepmother release her from the spell.

She had fought hardened army veterans on a daily basis, many of whom feared to look her in the eye. What was Jing to her? A woman, and a weak one at that. If Mai had to threaten her, then she would. Mai refused to fool the prince a minute longer.

She rose, straightening her spine so she stood at her full height. She was the hero of the siege of Dean, Mai reminded herself. She had served her Emperor with honour, and the Emperor himself had agreed to meet her. She would not be cowed by someone as insignificant as Jing.

Mai marched to her stepmother's apartment, which she now noticed was a fraction of the size of the one she shared with Yi. She found the place in a flurry of activity, with clothing flung everywhere before being packed into chests.

"You're leaving?" Mai blurted out.

"What are you doing here?" Jing asked irritably, glaring. "Have you come to gloat?"

Gloat? Mai faltered. What could she possibly have to gloat about? Jing had gotten her wish, that one of her girls would marry a prince.

"Save your breath," Jing advised. "There is no chance of the girls marrying now. Instead, we must go home and mourn."

Mai's breath caught in her throat. "Mourn who?"

"The great Yeong Fu, who surely could have held on another week so that he might see his daughters secure in marriage. Now…they will have nothing." Jing paused to bark instructions to Jia, who hurried off to fetch whatever it was Jing had asked for. "First the ancestors take my son, then they take my husband. Ah, I am cursed!"

Mai could scarcely believe it. "My…my father is

dead?"

"Yes, your father is dead. It's your fault for not being there to take care of him. He talked of nothing but you the week before we left," Jing snapped. "While you were off pretending to be some hero, your father was dying. Alone."

Mai didn't know what to say. All her fierce words and thoughts had dried up. Her father couldn't be gone. He couldn't be. She had promised her mother she'd take care of him, but she'd failed. Now, all she could do was burn incense in the shrine every day and beg both her mother and father to forgive her.

"I must go home," Mai found herself saying.

Jing gave a most unladylike snort. "Another useless mouth to feed that we can ill afford? What for?"

"I will come home for my father's funeral, as is proper," Mai said, finding strength in her sorrow. "I will honour his memory. And you cannot stop me." She drew herself up and returned Jing's glare with one of her own.

"Oh, by all that is holy…I refuse to be intimidated by a girl who thinks that because she looks like a man, she is better than me!" Jing bit down hard on her lip and waved her hand at Mai.

Mai felt a faint tingle run across her skin, and then the weight of her robes dragging on the ground because – she glanced down – all of a sudden, they did. She yanked up one sleeve, then the other, seeing her own arms for the first time in too long, instead of the muscled appendages she'd grown used to. Impetuously, she threw her arms around Jing. "Thank you!"

"Quickly, take those off. You must wear women's clothes, but not too fine, or someone will question why they did not see you before." Jing surveyed the room. "Jia! Find her something of yours."

What Mai suspected were Jia's only set of spare clothes were brought, and Mai put them on. The rough cloth was strange against her skin after the smooth silk of her court clothes, but Mai knew she would not wear the maid's clothes for long.

"I will go get my things," Mai said. "I won't be long."

"Be quick about it. We won't wait for you," Jing snapped.

Mai nodded and hurried off to the prince's apartments. Hopefully, he would be fast asleep and not notice a lowly maid going about her business.

Thirty-Four

Mai hesitated in the doorway to the prince's apartments. They seemed bigger somehow, though she knew they had not changed. Only she had changed.

No, she scolded herself. She had not changed at all. She had merely lost the illusion that made her appear to be something she wasn't.

A small part of her wanted the prince to be awake, to recognise her for who she was, and claim her as his bride, like Lady Zuleika had said. But she was too mired in her grief to let even that tiny ray of hope lighten her mood. Her father was dead, and she must return home to mourn him. She would never dance with him in the courtyard again, nor bring him his tea, nor pray with him in the shrine as they laid out her mother's favourite incense. She could never thank him for all that he had taught her, the invaluable skills which had kept her alive at the siege of Dean.

A light still burned in the prince's sitting room, as though he was not yet back from the ball. The light was more than enough to set her mother's shoes sparkling where they sat in pride of place on the table. Despite herself, Mai smiled. Sweet prince. He must have seen that she'd forgotten her shoes and brought them back here for her before rejoining the festivities.

With trembling hands, she reached for her mother's shoes, magically transformed into a dream she could no longer indulge in. But she could treasure the shoes, and the memories that came with them. Mai scooped up the slippers, cradling them like the precious heirlooms they were.

"Put those down!" Yi roared. "Get out!"

Startled, she dropped the shoes back on the table. Had he looked so big and fierce before? It did not matter – he was still Yi, the man she loved. A man she must say goodbye to, for even if he had offered to marry her, no wedding could take place until the mourning period for her father was over. Not even the Emperor himself would stop her from returning home for her father's funeral.

She sighed. "I must – " she began.

"Do you know who I am?" he interrupted.

What a peculiar question. Had Yi drunk too much baijiu, or was this some strange joke? Slowly, she nodded.

"Who am I?" he demanded.

It was on the tip of her tongue to tell him he was a puffed-up rooster who couldn't fight, but realisation dawned on her that he did not know who she was. Dressed like a maid, and a girl again, she would appear as a stranger to him.

Her mouth was dry as she replied, "His Highness, the Prince of Swords." As any palace servant would.

"And you would dare to steal from me?" he thundered.

"I wasn't!" she protested hotly, opening her mouth to tell him that they were not his shoes, but hers.

He seemed to read her mind. "Not another word, or I shall call the palace guards and have you thrown out."

Mai longed to tell him the truth, but she knew he meant what he said. If he summoned the palace guards, she would either end up in a fight where someone would get hurt, or she would have to let them throw her out. And Jing would leave without her.

Angrily, Mai met his gaze, determined to make him recognise her.

Recognition sparked in his eyes for a moment

before Yi turned away. "Tell whatever woman who sent you that I have chosen my bride and no trick or spell will change my mind. Now get out!"

Mai's heart broke. She was too late. Yi had chosen someone else. She had nowhere else to go but home. Tears sprang to her eyes – tears she refused to shed in front of Yi – so she turned away before he could see her heartbreak. What was losing a pair of shoes to losing the man she loved? Mai had nothing left, now, for as she departed from the prince's apartments for the final time, she left her bleeding heart on the table, beside her mother's shoes.

Thirty-Five

The next morning, Yi sent Heng to Yeong Fu's apartment to ask whether he might meet with the man over the course of the morning. Heng came hurrying back, wide-eyed. "The whole family has packed up and left. Apparently, Yeong Fu died suddenly and they all returned home for the funeral first thing this morning."

Yi's hand closed around the shoes on the table. So that was why Mao had not returned last night. He must have been with his family, and returned home with them for his father's funeral. As any dutiful son would do.

Surely he would have taken a moment to return

here to pack his belongings, and say farewell. Yet all of Mao's clothes were still in his room, and the shoes sat where he'd left them last night.

Now Yi remembered the maid from last night. Had she been sent to collect Mao's things, and give him a message from Mao? The more he thought about it, the more Yi decided it must be true. He shouldn't have frightened the girl away.

Mao was right. He should wait before he married one of Mao's sisters. Life in the army had left him with absolutely no idea how to deal with women.

Thinking about Mao, though, made him remember another important appointment. One he must keep, though Mao wouldn't.

His parents were breaking their fast when Yi entered their private courtyard, but his mother waved him in.

"Mother. Father." Yi bowed. "I have come to convey my deepest apologies for my friend, Yeong Mao. His father has died and he has returned home for the funeral."

"Your friend, the war hero?" Father asked.

"Yes."

"Who was his father again?" The Emperor reached for another slice of peach.

"Yeong Fu, the great general. His mother was Da Ying, the military strategist." Yi couldn't keep the grin off his face at those words.

Mother frowned. "Yeong Fu had no sons. Unless he fathered some on that girl...what was her name again? Jing?" She turned to her husband. "That witch girl you made him marry...oh, it must have been fourteen years ago now. He had no sons, so you commanded that he marry again. I saw her at court last night at the ball, with her two girls. She'd magicked them to look older, and dressed them in purple and gold, the imperial colours, as if they were already members of our household." Delicately, she bit into an egg.

Yi found himself shaking his head. "No, that's not possible. I've seen him fight. His military tactics and strategies are second to none. He makes me look like an idiot, and he can beat me in a fight before I can blink. He carried me out of Dean on his own back when I was wounded. He told me who his parents were, and his father trained him in war since he was a child. His mother is Da Ying, I swear it, not some witch. I have shared a tent with the man for the whole of the siege, and my apartments here since we arrived at the palace. I know him, and he cannot be anything except who he says he is!"

"Calm yourself," Mother said. She nodded at Yi. "What is that in your hand? Is that a token from your bride, so that you do not forget her?"

Yi glanced down. In his hand, he still clutched Mao's shoes. He could not even remember picking them up. "No," he said slowly. "I picked these up in the garden, after we finished sparring. I thought they were Mao's, but…"

Mother held out her hand and Yi wordlessly gave her the shoes.

"Beautiful," she purred. "Very well made. I have never seen any of our shoemakers do work like this, though they are silk. And the glass beads! Why, every one of them looks like it has been cut by a knife, so sharply that they shatter the very light that touches them. Whoever makes your friend's shoes would have an honoured place in court, if they so wished it."

"They're not…" Yi began, but then he stopped. He had seen Mao wearing these shoes. His mother's eyes were knowing. "Did you see Mao wear these to the ball, too?"

Mother inclined her head. "Indeed I did. I wanted to ask who made them, for they look better suited for a woman than a man, and perhaps now we will never know." She eyed them. "But if your friend no longer wants them, I would like them."

"No!" Yi snatched the shoes back and hugged them to his chest. "He left them behind in his hurry to attend his father's funeral. I must return them to him."

"Convey our condolences to your friend, and to

Yeong Fu's widow," Mother said. "They were married for fourteen years. I am sure she is quite bereft without him, even if their story was not the stuff of legends, like the tales of Fu and Da Ying."

Fourteen years. Mao had said his sisters were younger than that. Ordinary girls who danced and…were not Da Ying's daughters. His heart sank. So much for finding a bride with Mao's help.

"The stories say they fell in love during a campaign, but the General forbade them to see one another. She dressed in armour and marched into battle at Fu's side anyway, and when he fell in battle, she took command of his troops and won a great victory." Mother smiled. "What the stories do not say is that she was pregnant with his child at the time, and that night she went into labour early, and gave birth to a daughter. Born in the heart of battle. What an empress she would make."

Yi stared at his mother in confusion. "You mean…Mao has another sister? One who did not dance at the ball last night?"

Mother shrugged "Did she not? I did not notice every girl there. There were so many. But when you said you chose one of Fu's daughters for your bride, of course I assumed it was Da Ying's girl. The others are merely children."

Yi's head whirled. Women's shoes. No sons. Born in battle. Another sister.

Only one thing he knew for certain: the answers to all his questions lay with Mao, and Mao alone. If he wanted to know the truth, he must ask Mao.

Yi bowed to his mother and father, thanking them for their time, before heading back to his apartments.

If Mao had left the palace, Yi would go after him. One way or the other, he would know the truth. Either Mao had not been honest about whose son he was…or Mao was no one's son at all, but a daughter.

Yi would journey to Mao's house and find the daughter born in battle, and make her put on Mao's shoes. If they fit, he would ask her to dance for him, just like the other girls had last night.

If the girl truly was Mao, he would know.

And if she was…Yi swore he would make Da Ying's daughter his bride.

Thirty-Six

When Yeong Fu's funeral was ended, Mai busied herself in the kitchen, doing the dishes to keep herself busy. After her father's death, many of his loyal servants had left, for they weren't as fond of Jing and there was plenty of work to do on the farms of the village. With all the men who had gone to war and not yet returned, every pair of hands were needed to till and seed the fields in the hope of a summer harvest.

Like most soldiers, she had learned the use of a cookfire and the kitchen here was no different, if a little more civilised. On the days when the cook didn't come, Mai had to use her cooking skills, to Jing's loud complaints. Mai closed her ears to them. She had eaten worse food prepared by the army cooks, and though it was nowhere near as palatable as palace fare, it was edible enough. As long as they had food, her family would not starve.

On laundry day, Mai found herself alone, without a single servant to help, as a plague of birds had descended on the fields and they needed every spare person to either scare the birds away or replant the seeds they had eaten. She worked all day and into the night, washing clothes and linen, before hanging it all out to dry in the yard. She might have returned Jia's clothes, but she had taken the girl's place in what had increasingly become Jing's house. The only place Mai truly felt her mother and father's presence was the shrine, now, where she had barely a moment to light a stick of incense for each of them before she had to start her chores for the day.

The one thing from her earlier life she did not relinquish was her predawn dance, though now she performed it alone. There was no one to fight or spar with, and there never would be again. The baby brother who had died shortly before his father would never grow to adulthood, so Mai was the closest thing their household of women had to a protector. She might no longer look like a man, but she was most certainly a match for one.

So every day she kept herself in readiness for an

army she never expected to arrive.

But as fate would have it, the morning after laundry day, it did.

Thirty-Seven

The further away they travelled from the capital, the more each mountain lake reminded Yi of Mao. At first, it was just because they all seemed to be the same shade of blue green as Mao's court clothes in one of the saddlebags, until he found himself thinking almost constantly of his former roommate. Could the man he'd known truly have been a woman all this time?

The erotic dreams had returned, featuring a woman whose face he still could not see, but Yi no longer woke up in horror when he saw Mao's face or heard his voice in his dreams. Instead, he wondered whether Mao was simply a particularly muscular girl with a deep voice and a homely face who had chosen to join the army because she feared she would never be beautiful enough to attract a husband.

There were days he did not want to believe that Mao could be a woman, too. They were becoming fewer and fewer, though, especially when he remembered the knowing look in his mother's eyes as she'd held Mao's shoes. She had also mentioned Mao's stepmother being a witch. Yi hadn't met one before, though he had heard of them. Perhaps she had cursed her beautiful stepdaughter so that she merely looked like a man. If so, Yi would demand she break the curse as part of the marriage agreement, for he would not take a cursed bride.

Yi rode through the gates of the house, entering a courtyard filled with linens blowing in the wind as they dried, but no one was in sight. He dismounted, handing the reins of his horse to Heng, and telling his men to wait in the yard. If his mother was right, this was now a household of women, and women in mourning. He had no wish to frighten them by bringing an invading army into their home.

Someone emerged from the house and stood on the veranda, clad in white. From the quality of her mourning robes as well as her age, Yi judged her to be Fu's widow.

"Mistress Yeong," he said, bowing. "I have come to see your son, Yeong Mao, and to return his things, which he left at the palace."

"I am Mistress Yeong," the woman said weakly. "But I no longer have a son." She buried her face in her hands and burst into noisy tears.

A crying woman. What in the ancestors' name was he supposed to do with one of those?

Heng slid down from his horse and advanced to stand at Yi's shoulder. "Mistress Yeong, may we come inside to speak with you? We have travelled a long way and would like some refreshment."

"Yes…yes." She seemed to collect herself at Heng's words, and beckoned them inside.

Heng grabbed Yi's arm before he could follow her inside. "She's a witch," Heng said softly. "She has an illusion about her, making her look younger and prettier than she is. Watch her if she bites her lip, or otherwise does something to draw blood, for blood fuels her spells."

One day, Yi intended to ask Heng how he knew all this. For now, though, he simply nodded, before heading inside the house.

Thirty Eight

The sound of hooves on the stone gateway woke Mai from her uncomfortable sleep. She had spent so long dealing with the laundry last night that she'd laid down by the embers of the fireplace, with a rice bag as her pillow, to get a little sleep before dawn. Somehow the rice bag had come open as she slept, though, and the ashes were full of rice grains. With the last harvest as poor as it had been, Mai had shared much of their spare food with the villagers, and this was their last bag of rice. Every grain was valuable.

Sighing at her own stupidity for spilling the stuff, she began sifting through the ashes for the grains of rice so she could return them to the bag. She soon forgot about horses, visitors or anything outside the fireplace until Lei burst into the kitchen.

"Mai, Mai! You must make tea. The prince is here, and he is looking for a boy. Mother keeps telling him our brother is dead, but he does not believe her. He goes on and on about how our brother bought one of his sisters a gift, but how it belonged to a girl with big feet. He keeps holding up his hands to show how big." Lei held her hands apart, much wider than her own bound feet. "You must make tea, and when you serve it, he shall see your feet and stop hounding Mother. Every time she tells him her son is dead, she cries, but he only grows angrier. The courtyard is full of men. I am afraid he will hurt Mother."

The rice could wait. Mai had not gone to war so that some lackey from the Emperor could torment her family. She still seethed at how rude Yi had been to her when she'd come to his apartments to collect her shoes. She'd teach him a lesson in manners no matter how many men he'd brought. How dare he!

She clambered to her feet, brushing the ashes from her white robe. Not so white now, but it mattered little. She could still best Yi in rags or court robes.

"But the tea!" Lei hissed.

"Men who invade a house of mourning without an invitation do not deserve tea," Mai said, striding through the home where she had once been happy.

Jing's sitting room had grown shabby, but today she barely noticed it. Mai stood as tall and proud as the Empress herself at the entrance to Jing's sitting room and set her hands on her hips. "Who demands to see Yeong Mao?"

Heng shot to his feet, bowing before his knees had fully straightened, but Yi was slower to move, letting his gaze rake over Mai's body as he rose. His eyebrows rose a little, as if in surprise, but his slight smile said he liked what he saw.

Mai didn't give a rat's arse what he thought.

"Yeong Mao died on the road home from the capital. He broke his neck when his horse threw him. There was nothing anyone could do to save him. He walks with the ancestors now, including his father, and if you wish to see him, you are welcome to join them."

Yi looked stunned, but he recovered quickly.

Rooster, Mai thought, as she saw that arrogant look in his eye again. She longed to spar with him and throw him in the dust until that's all he could taste.

"Do you know who I am, girl?" he asked.

Mai could have kissed him for repeating the line he'd used the night of the ball. She'd relived that night so many times in her head, the correct response tripped off her tongue.

"Many call you the Prince of Swords, but Yeong Mao called you a rooster, with good reason, I think,"

Mai replied, ignoring Jing's horrified gasp. "Do you know who I am?"

The surprise took longer to leave his face this time. "The Empress spoke of a girl born in battle, the daughter of Yeong Fu and Da Ying. I believe she might be you, and if that's true, then I have something which belongs to you."

Mai folded her arms. "A gift from my brother?" She had fought in a war, not bought gifts for her sisters, let alone herself. She itched to catch Yi in a lie so she could ask him his true purpose here.

"Perhaps," he said. "I left it in my saddlebag."

Outside, where he had reinforcements, Mai added in her head. As if Yi suspected he might need them. That brought her up short. Did he truly know who she was?

She shot him a startled glance, but he wore an enigmatic smile that revealed nothing.

"Then lead the way," she said, gesturing, and he did.

She counted a dozen men and horses in the courtyard, their hooves leaving divots in her training circle that she would need to smooth over before tomorrow morning's dancing session. Mai bet Yi never let horses muck up his training yard.

Yi reached into his saddlebag and pulled out a parcel shrouded in purple silk. He unwrapped it slowly, drawing out every moment as though he enjoyed having her eyes on him. From the first glimpse, she knew what he held, though, so that when he finally held up her shoes in all their dazzling splendour, she could feign indifference despite the awed gasps from his men. Only Heng and Yi seemed immune – for both had seen them before.

"What do you think?" Yi asked.

"I think those are my mother's shoes," Mai replied. She suppressed a grin at Yi's shock. "I would need to see them more closely to be sure, but I am almost certain they are the same."

"You will! You must try them on. I insist!"

Mai waited while Heng brought her a bench to sit on, before Yi knelt at her feet.

"Your Highness, let me – " Heng began, but Yi waved him away.

"I must know that they fit!" Yi hissed. "I must know!" He took hold of her foot, and slipped on one shoe.

As Mai knew it would, the shoe fitted as though it was made for her, as indeed it was.

Yi gazed up at her searchingly. "Is it true?" he asked, half under his breath. The longing in his eyes made her wonder if he was going to kiss her.

Mai met his gaze and said nothing.

He cupped her other foot in his hand. For a long moment, he hesitated, before he finally slid on the second shoe.

"A perfect fit," he breathed. He pointed a shaking finger in Jing's direction. "Is that your mother?"

Mai laughed. "No, Jing is my stepmother, foisted on my father by the Emperor, who likes to breed more good men from the ones he has. I am the daughter of Da Ying." She dropped her voice so low only Yi would hear it. "But I think you already knew that."

She fancied that he nodded slightly, but she could not be certain.

"It is not enough that the shoes fit you," Yi announced. "Before I make my decision, you must dance."

Mai didn't like the sound of that. "What decision?"

He gave a slight shake of his head.

By the ancestors, he was putting on a show. Mai would not stand for it. "What decision?" she demanded.

He grabbed her arm and pulled her forward, until she dropped to her knees in the dirt. Mai heard the sound of steel scraping its way out of a scabbard. The touch of his sword was cold against her throat.

"Whether you should live or die," Yi said.

Thirty-Nine

She was so pretty, Yi's heart sang when he first beheld her. Maybe even beautiful, though it was hard to tell with her face smudged in soot. Her white robes were every bit as fine as those worn by the mistress of the house, though Yi fancied hers curved more at the chest than the older woman's did.

If this was Mao's sister, he would knock Yi down for thinking of her breasts. If the girl was Mao herself…would she knock him down or let him touch them? He caught himself smiling at the thought, and tried to smother it quickly. Not soon enough, though – the girl had seen, and it lit a furious fire in her eyes.

She repeated the same story the other woman –

Jing? – had told him, of Mao breaking his neck in a fall. That Yi could not believe. No one could recover from a fall quite as well as Mao. But if he was not here, then the girl had to be one and the same.

She knew him, that was certain, and she knew Mao's nickname for him, too. That meant nothing, though – if he was her brother, he might have told her that and many things about his life in the army and at court.

The shoes would give him his answer. If they fitted her, then she must be Mao, just as his mother had hinted.

A bench was brought, and Yi knelt at the girl's feet, longing for the shoes to fit and yet dreading what it would mean if they did.

He'd never felt so nervous in his life. With Mao, everything had been easy. As friends and brothers in arms, he'd always spoken freely. Yet this woman regarded him with barely concealed contempt.

Heng stepped forward, offering to help, but Yi waved him away. He had to do this. He had to fit the shoes to her feet with his own hands, so that he would know if they were hers. If she had sat on the dais beside him at the ball, fought with him every day, slept beside him at night…

Ancestors. Had he been dreaming of her while he slept beside her?

Yi swallowed and looked down. Somehow, without realising it, he'd put the shoes on her feet.

"A perfect fit," he breathed. He didn't want to believe it.

Perhaps she wasn't Da Ying's daughter. Or she wasn't Mao. Even as he voiced his doubts, she put them to rest. She was everything he could ever want in a bride, and more.

Except he had not seen her fight. That would be the final proof. Surely no woman could fight like Mao. No man alive could fight like Mao, and definitely no woman could.

He pulled her to her feet and she didn't resist. Did that mean she trusted him, or simply that she was docile? Yi couldn't be sure. He released her, and she landed neatly on her knees. Coincidence, perhaps. Or design.

He wanted to challenge her to a fight, but he would only look foolish in front of his men. The Prince of Swords, challenge a girl on her knees? But if he closed his eyes and imagined the kneeling figure was Mao…

Yi dragged his sword out of its scabbard, his hand resisting every inch of the way. Drawing his sword on a defenceless, unarmed, kneeling woman was dishonourable. She had done nothing wrong, except maybe lie to him. Either she was Mao, and she would laugh at him for daring to draw his sword, or she was

Mao's sister, and threatening her would bring the man himself out of hiding. Yi prayed that he was right as he held the blade to her silky throat and threatened her life.

He thought he heard her sigh, and her shoulders slumped the slightest bit. That was all the warning he had before she swept his legs out from under him and snatched the sword out of his hand.

His men drew their weapons, forming a circle that closed in slowly. Uncertainty showed on their faces – none of them wanted to go up against an opponent who could best the Prince of Swords. Why, he was the best swordsman in the kingdom, or so they said.

They were wrong. The best was Mao.

"You wish to dance with me, Prince of Swords?" she asked. "I will dance with you, but on one condition. We dance alone."

A victory, of sorts, thought Yi, as he clambered to his feet. He nodded. "Yes. All of you, sheathe your weapons. Except you. " He pointed at the nearest man. "Hand me your sword. She's going to borrow mine for a moment."

One man sniggered, and the others followed suit. Tension ebbed away from the circle as his men realised what their eyes could already see: their prince in a sparring circle with a girl holding a sword. She was not Mao to them. As for Yi…he wasn't sure what she was to him. His best friend. His best friend's sister. Maybe his bride. If she'd have him.

Doubt crept in. What if she wouldn't?

Weapons slid back into scabbards until the only two naked blades were the one in his hand and the one in hers.

"Shall we dance?" he asked, bowing slightly as he held his sword in readiness.

Her whole face lit up with a smile so dazzling Yi's heart stopped. There was no woman in the world he wanted more.

"We shall," she said, taking a fighting stance.

Forty

It had been weeks since Mai had sparred properly with anyone, so it was impossible to keep the smile from her face as she crossed swords with Yi. Though they carried true steel and not wooden practice swords this time, she was reminded of the night of the ball, when they had circled and danced for what might have been hours as they lost track of the time. Then as now, they had matched one another perfectly. This was neither a fight nor a battle. It truly was a dance.

A dance she wanted to continue forever.

Mai faltered at the thought. She did not dare lift her hopes so high – she knew better now. She might not know why the prince was here, but it could not be to claim her as his bride. Why, he had seen her feet – shod them himself. He knew she did not have proper lotus feet like a court lady.

So this dance must end, she told herself. Much like the siege of Dean, it would only end when there was a victor. But first, they must fight.

"What will you give me if I win this fight?" she asked suddenly.

Several of Yi's men laughed. Mai did not blame them. After all, they were loyal to their prince, and she was a girl they did not know. Of course they believed his victory was assured.

Yi stared at her for a moment. "I will give you whatever you wish," he said finally.

Your heart, her own heart screamed in her chest, but Mai ignored it. The prince could not be hers. "I wish that you would place my family under your protection, so that they do not fear the Emperor's armies or that of our neighbours. And return the men who left for the siege of Dean, for the siege is over now, yet they have not returned."

He nodded once.

"And when the prince wins?" one of the onlookers called. "What will you give him, girl?"

Mai had already given him her heart. She had nothing else left to give. "If you win, what would you ask of me?" she asked Yi.

His dark eyes regarded hers for a moment that stretched for far too long.

Then he moved, advancing in a flurry of blows, just as he had on the day they met.

Mai blocked every blow, letting him get closer to her with each one until he was near enough to lean over and whisper into her ear, "I would ask you to be my bride, daughter of Da Ying."

His answer surprised her. Surely she could not have heard right. Yet even as she watched him, he nodded and mouthed one more word: "Mine."

There were many paths to victory, as Mai well knew.

Mai looked deep into his eyes, though two swords separated them, and chose her path.

Forty-One

It was as though time stood still, ready to repeat itself. Yi stood in this courtyard, fighting the woman in white, yet at the same time, he stood in the dust outside Dean, expecting to beat Mao, only to find himself defeated. He lunged, leaving himself open to whatever rapid defence Mao had used on him that first time. Now he would know for sure whether this woman was Mao or someone else entirely.

Her eyes met his, as if she could read his thoughts. She twisted, just as Mao had done, but instead of throwing him to the ground, the girl slipped and landed flat on her back. Defeated, as Yi brought the tip of his sword to her throat.

Her gaze was as tranquil as one of the mountain lakes he'd passed to reach her home. "Victory is yours, my prince," she murmured.

His heart sank like a stone. No. He didn't want to be victorious. He wanted Mao. This had to be him…her. But he had never beaten Mao in a fight. Never. So this girl with Mao's eyes couldn't be…

"Leave us," he said. When no one obeyed, he repeated, much louder this time, "Leave us!"

His men retreated out the gate while the Yeong household headed back into the house. Where they could all spy on him and the girl, Yi presumed. He hoisted the girl to her feet and dragged her into the nearest building – her ancestral shrine, he realised, once they were inside. A fitting place to execute her, if that was his wish, but if he killed her, any answers she might have died with her.

The strange girl didn't struggle in the slightest, letting him manhandle her into the place without a murmur. Did she want to die?

He released her, expecting her to stumble, but she merely straightened her spine, then remembered herself and bowed her head.

"You're not Mao," Yi said bitterly.

"I told you, Yeong Mao died on the road between the palace and home," she said.

"Then where is his funeral tablet, so that I might

burn some incense for his spirit?" Yi demanded. "I owe him my life, and if he is dead, I cannot repay my debt."

The girl swallowed, looking uncomfortable for the first time. "He has none. Nor will he, while I yet live."

"But you are not Mao!" Yi repeated.

She smiled sadly. "No, I am not. I am Yeong Mai, the daughter of Yeong Fu and Da Ying. Victor of the siege of Dean and every bout I have fought against you. Mao was an illusion cast to allow a woman to join the army in her father's place, to save her family. This I have done with honour. I should be content."

"You didn't win that fight out there, and that is why I know you can't be Mao!" Yi said. Mao had perfect balance. Mao would never have slipped…especially not in those magical shoes.

"Because I did not tip you on your royal behind as I did during our first sparring match, and countless times after? You'll never be a good fighter, Rooster, unless you truly master the art of war. I have already won a victory that way. Once I have won, I do not repeat my tactics but respond to circumstances in a variety of ways. A good general is not a predictable one." She stepped close so he could feel her breath on his face as she looked up at him. "Who says I did not win?"

Ancestors help him, Yi wanted to kiss her. To grab

this woman with both hands and plunder those lecturing lips until he forgot what she'd said. Until she forgot, too. He forced himself to step back. "Me. I mean, you didn't win. You slipped. I saw you."

"I lay down, with my sword in hand," she corrected, showing him her sheathed blade. Huh. She must have put her sword away as he dragged her across the yard. "It does not follow that because I am victorious, you are not." She gestured toward the courtyard. "And it is not seemly that a prince should be defeated by a girl in front of his own men. You offered a victory more tempting than the one I had planned for, which I choose to accept."

"You choose to…" Nothing made sense any more. Least of all the thoughts in Yi's head. "What do you accept?"

The girl – Mai, Yi reminded himself – licked her lips nervously. "You said if you won, you would take me for your bride. My sisters would consider a prince for a husband to be the ultimate victory. Though I don't often agree with them, this time…I might." Her eyes seemed to dance, though the rest of her stood still, anticipating…something.

Mai or Mao or whoever she was had more pride than the Emperor himself. Yi laughed. "You might consider me a suitable victory prize?"

Mai tilted her head as she scrutinised him. "Your

body is sound, and your mind is mostly so. Your sense of humour and manners are charming enough. But you are a terrible fighter. A girl could beat you, Rooster." When she smiled like that, so full of mischief, Yi almost saw Mao in her face…but…she was much prettier than Mao.

"You could beat me?" he asked, assuming a fighting stance. "If you wish to spar again, we will, but the outcome will be the same."

Her smile didn't fade. "I will still win, but without witnesses, you might not." She beckoned him to attack.

Yi strode forward and…

…somehow found himself lying on the cold tiles, gasping for the breath his fall had knocked out of him as his sword clattered against the far wall, out of reach.

Gentle feminine laughter greeted him and he glared up at Mai's joyful face. "Are you happy now, my prince? I can teach you how to fight as I do, you know. My father taught me everything he knew, and I will share it with you. You only have to ask. I know a courtyard in the palace where we can dance together daily, if that is your wish." She held out a delicate hand to help him to his feet.

She couldn't lift him, so Yi waved away her offer of assistance and clambered to his feet on his own. "Mao…"

"Mai," she corrected.

"Mai," he repeated. Even her name on his tongue tasted sweet. "All those nights we shared a tent, I dreamed of a woman I could not see. A woman who held my heart in her hands every moment I was with her. Yet when I tried to see her, all I saw was my roommate, Mao. His face would shock me awake, every time, because when I looked upon him, I felt no desire at all. And now I look at you…and I wonder…"

"I did not dream of you," she admitted slowly. "But when Heng helped me into my armour, I wished it was you." She blushed. "And when we fought together, melee style, I often stood closer to you than necessary, so that I might brush against you during the fight."

"I did not want a bride," he began.

"And I never wished to be one," she finished. "Yet when you offered…" Her eyes grew very wide and dark. Mountain lakes a man could get lost in, if he wasn't careful.

What was he saying? Yi was already lost, a long time ago. "Be mine, Yeong Mai," he said softly. "I cannot send a matchmaker to ask your father for your hand, so I must ask you here, before your ancestral spirits. Will you be my bride, though I am such a terrible fighter, even an orphan girl could beat me? I will endeavour to protect you, and your family, as best I can. Mao was the best friend a man could ever have, but I would ask for more from you, Mai. I want you to be my friend and my lover, as I will be yours. I owe you my life, and I will give it to you freely, one day at a time, every day I have, until we join our ancestors in the spirit realm."

Her eyes held wonder, but also warmth. "I will." A tiny smile teased him. "But first give me a taste of what to expect. I know the quality of your friendship, and what kind of dancer you are, but I am new to love."

She wanted him to make love to her here, in her ancestral shrine? Yi swallowed. "Would a kiss do? A taste?"

She nodded once. "Perhaps." Mai stood calmly with her hands by her sides, waiting.

For him, Yi realised. She had always insisted he attack first, and this was no different. She would judge his kiss the way she judged his fighting. His heart grew cold. What if she found him wanting?

"Are you as experienced at kissing as you are at fighting?" he blurted out.

Her calm evaporated. "I…have never…"

A girl who could put a grown man on his arse as easily as breathing wouldn't have been the victim of stolen kisses, Yi realised. It was a lucky man who could touch her at all.

The thought gave him courage, bolstered by the panic in her eyes. He would protect her and take care of her.

Yi raised his hands to show he was unarmed, then closed the distance between them in two strides. One hand grasped her shoulder – gently, for she was far more delicate than Mao – as he lifted his other hand to her face. Still he hesitated. He didn't want to mess this up, not least because he'd end up flat on his back on the floor if he did.

He traced her lips with his thumb. They were softer and plumper than he'd imagined, even in his dreams. Kissing her would be…

She bit his thumb. Gently, but just enough to sting.

"When campaigning, be swift as the wind," Mai whispered. "Do you wish to fight for my heart, or not, Rooster?"

He remembered the words, for he had heard her say them before the start of every fight. "Plunder like fire, stand as firm as the mountains, and move like a thunderbolt."

His fingers tangled in her hair as he pressed his mouth to hers, lightning-fast. Swift enough to steal the breeze of her breath as she gasped, parting her lips just wide enough to let his tongue plunder her mouth. Desire blazed inside him as her arms wrapped around him, so that her body pressed against his so firmly he wanted to topple them both to the tiles and make love to her then and there. He didn't want just her heart, he wanted her whole body, too, for she had ensnared his spirit so completely he was bound to her already.

After an eternity that was still too short, Mai broke the kiss, laying her head against his heaving chest. "I like your fire, my prince. And you are…quite firm." She was pressed so tightly against him, she couldn't help but feel his arousal.

Yi reddened. "I will control myself until you are no longer in mourning, and we are married," he said.

Mai laughed. "I meant the muscles of your chest, but yes, that one feels firm, too. Like you desire me, even though…I am like this." She gestured at her body.

His gaze followed her waving hand and his desire burned brighter still. "How could I feel anything else? You are not just the most beautiful woman I have ever seen. I have fought at your side, when I should have spent every day fighting for you. You hold my heart, Mai, and you always will." He inhaled some of the incense smoke which made him cough, spoiling the effect of his words.

"It seems my mother's spirit approves," Mai said, pointing at the offending incense. "My father knows better than to go against her wishes. My heart is yours, when you choose to claim it."

Now, his heart urged, but Yi resisted. The girl was still mourning her father, and they could not marry until her mourning period was past. "I choose to claim it now with a kiss, and a promise that the day your mourning ends, I shall have the rest of you, too."

As his arms slipped around her waist, pulling her in close, she said, "You will, my prince," before he silenced her with a soul-consuming kiss.

Forty-Two

The wedding formalities seemed to take an eternity. When Yi escorted her to yet another chamber, Mai swore that if she was forced to drink another cup of tea, she was going to accidentally spill it down her robes so that she could excuse herself to change clothes. If it weren't for Yi at her side, she would have heartily refused to marry at all by the end of the first hour. As it was, she gritted her teeth, kept her eyes lowered and imagined the calm mountain lake beside her family home.

Yi closed the doors behind them. "Would you like some tea?" he offered.

Mai whirled, ready to tell him exactly what she

thought of tea, only to discover him grinning with a bottle in his hand.

"Because my family or the servants have only left us this fine bottle of baijiu to drink. No tea at all," Yi finished.

Mai relaxed enough to laugh a little. "If that is anywhere near as good as what we were drinking on the night of the ball, then yes."

Yi unstoppered the bottle with a satisfying pop. He held it to his nose and inhaled deeply. "As I suspected. My father has given us a bottle of his best, to celebrate."

He found two cups and poured the clear liquor into them. Mai reached for the nearest one, but Yi stopped her. "Wait. This is strong stuff. Before we have any, I must make certain I married a woman, and not a man."

Mai raised her hands to remove her veil, but Yi stopped her again.

"Please. I have dreamed about this moment." He laughed nervously. "Usually it's good, and you are a beautiful woman, but sometimes I see the man who knocked me to the ground so many times in training."

"I did not knock you down," Mai replied. "You lost your balance and fell, more often than not because you did not see a blow coming. You should be more observant."

"Tonight, I will be," he promised, reaching for her. Carefully, he lifted the veil from her head. "Such beautiful hair. I must see it free, as it was the day you bested me in the courtyard of your ancestral home."

She helped him unpin her hair, so that it cascaded down her back.

"So beautiful," he breathed, stroking her hair.

No one had ever touched her like this before. Mai closed her eyes, finally understanding why her stepmother's cat purred when she stroked it. If Mai could purr, she would definitely do so when Yi stroked her like this.

She wanted to protest when he stopped, but his hands had moved to her front, untying her robe, so he could slip it off her shoulders, leaving her clad only in her underskirt.

Yi's eyes shone with admiration. "To think I bathed beside you a thousand times, and shared a tent with you for countless nights, and yet I never saw these sweet breasts. You are right. I should have been more observant."

Mai felt her cheeks grow hot as he continued to stare at her chest. "You definitely did not bathe with me a thousand times. A hundred, or maybe two, but you avoided bathing for days at a time. I bathed a thousand times, morning and night, and sometimes after a hard training session. I may have pretended to be a man, but I could not tolerate smelling like one."

"You have always smelled like paradise," Yi admitted. "Sometimes, I wondered what was wrong with me, for I would wake many a morning filled with desire, and yet when I opened my eyes I would see Mao, a man I did not desire at all. Yet now, it all makes sense, and I cannot resist." He cupped her breasts reverently, bowing to kiss each one.

Mai gasped at his touch, wanting to beg for more but too nervous to say a word. She swallowed, and made her decision. She unfastened her underskirt and let that fall, stepping out of her shoes so she stood naked before him. "This is the body you bathed with, and lay on the pallet beside you when we shared a tent. I am smaller than Mao, and softer, but I wear the same scars. I – "

Yi trailed a line of kisses down her shoulder. "I fought at your side as you gained every one of them. And to think I allowed Heng to dress you in your armour, when it could have been my hands on you every day. I only wish I could have protected you from war the way a man is supposed to protect his wife. I promise you will never have to fight another battle for as long as I live."

"Only if you do not fight any, either," she countered. "For the best swordsman in the empire, you have needed to be saved a lot." She smiled. "But if

I go to war again at your side, your hands alone will help me with my armour. You don't know how many times I wished it was you instead of Heng."

Yi bowed. "As my lady wishes, if duty and the Emperor allow."

Duty. It was their duty to consummate this marriage, and Mai had longed for this for…longer than she liked to admit. "Right now, your duty is to disrobe for your wife," Mai said, more nervous than she expected.

She had seen him naked so many times, she could trace every scar from memory. Yet now he was her husband, and that fierce warrior body would join with hers, her heart danced in her chest in anticipation. Eager anticipation.

Now he was the one who hesitated. "I have more scars than you. Some from our last battle which have not completely healed. If you expected a husband who is handsome and whole, I am no longer that man. The scars on my back…"

"My prince, I will know and love every scar, for as you say, I fought at your side as you gained every one of them," Mai said. She unfastened Yi's robes, baring him to the waist as they fell to the floor. She moistened her lips nervously, then reached for the cord holding his pants up and untied that, too. Trying not to think about how they were both naked, she forced herself to walk around him, taking note of every scar from the faded lines on his shins through to the badly-healed burns on his back. She couldn't help laying her hand on the shiny skin. "Does it still hurt?" she murmured.

"No, and with your hands on me like that, I would burn again, just to feel your touch," Yi said.

"My hands are yours to command, my prince," she replied. "After all, you won the fight, and you have yet to claim your prize."

"I want to claim you, but you are no prize," he said, pulling her hard against him when she opened her mouth to protest. "You are the reason I will fight my whole life long, so that I can keep you, and keep you safe. For I could stand losing each and every city in the kingdom, and even the throne itself, but I would not survive losing you. I love you, Mai, my dancer, my balance, and all the honour and glory a man could hope for. All I can offer in return is myself, as your prince."

Her prince. Yes. Holding tight to him, she backed him toward the bed until she tripped him and he tipped backward onto the mattress. Yi didn't let go of her, so she landed on top of him, blissfully aware of his hard, naked body beneath her.

Remembering the bold camp followers she'd envied so long ago, Mai sat up, straddling Yi's hips. She drew in a deep breath and drove her hips down, taking his length inside her. She gasped at the strange fullness, but it felt so right that it was but a moment before she started to move, riding him like she'd wanted to for so long.

"Mai...oh, ancestors, Mai!" he cried, grasping her hips as he thrust into her, matching her rhythm perfectly.

Balance. This was balance, the transcendental dance of two lovers so perfect for each other that when they joined, the rest of the world fell away.

And then the balance tipped, sending Mai's very soul flying to the heavens as she cried out for joy. Yet as she flew, Yi's arms held her securely, as his matching cry rang out across the sky. They flew together as one.

Mingled, joyous sounds that would ring in her ears for ever after, as Yi made her happy, again and again. Finally, Mai understood the fairy tales, knowing that if anyone got to live as happily ever after as her and her prince, then they were fortunate indeed.

Author's Note

If you're looking for more fairy tale retellings…here's a sneak peek from *Revel Twelve Dancing Princesses Retold*, the next book in the series.

Bonus Sneak Peek

Revel: Twelve Dancing Princesses Retold

"We should have made the wedding this week," Dokia said, lacing her fingers through Vasco's. "Waiting eight more days is torture."

"I call it delicious anticipation," Vasco replied. "Besides, if we got married this week, we wouldn't have a house to live in. Tomorrow I'll make a start on the roof, so that when you become my bride, we'll be able to spend our wedding night under a roof."

She lifted her gaze to the sky and sighed. "Right now, I would be perfectly happy with the stars as my roof, the night I become yours. If I have you, I will have everything I ever wanted."

"Right up until it rains," Vasco said.

Dokia laughed. "And that is why you're my lord and provider, or you will be, after next week. I cannot think of rain while the sun still shines."

"Ah, but the sun is setting now. And once the sun is gone, I'll make sure that all you can think about is you and me." Vasco raced into the trees, pulling her along until they reached the clearing they had claimed as their own.

Kissing Dokia was like air – he couldn't get enough of her. Their kisses grew more heated, and their clothes began to loosen before they started removing them entirely.

Vasco laid her on the soft grass by the stream, where she gazed up at him with eyes full of love.

"With all the practice we're getting, you will be perfect at this when our wedding night comes," she teased.

"Only because you are already perfect, my Eudocia," Vasco said, kicking off his boots.

"Flatterer," she replied, undoing the lacing of her gown to expose most of her chest. "What about these? Perfect enough for you?"

"Too perfect for me," Vasco replied. "Much like the rest of you. I don't know what madness made you accept me, but before you recover your senses, I will accept anything you offer me."

She parted her gown completely, laying herself bare. "I offer you everything I am, and everything I have. Take me, Vasco."

Vasco opened his mouth to respond, but another voice cut in, "That's a mighty pretty morsel. Too pretty for some peasant boy."

Something crashed into the side of Vasco's head and he fell lifeless to the grass. He never heard Dokia's screams pierce the air, or those from the village as it burned. When he awoke, there was nothing but silence and death to greet him.

For hours he walked the ruins of his home, looking for hope where there was none. So he did what any young man would after everything he had known was dead and buried: he joined the army, figuring that death would find him soon enough.

But fate had a different plan for Vasco.

The tale continues in the next book in the series
Revel:
Twelve Dancing Princesses Retold

About the Author

Demelza Carlton has always loved the ocean, but on her first snorkelling trip she found she was afraid of fish.

She has since swum with sea lions, sharks and sea cucumbers and stood on spray drenched cliffs over a seething sea as a seven-metre cyclonic swell surged in, shattering a shipwreck below.

Demelza now lives in Perth, Western Australia, the shark attack capital of the world.

The *Ocean's Gift* series was her first foray into fiction, followed by her suspense thriller *Nightmares* trilogy. She swears the *Mel Goes to Hell* series ambushed her on a crowded train and wouldn't leave her alone.

Want to know more? You can follow Demelza on Facebook, Twitter, YouTube or her website, Demelza Carlton's Place at:

www.demelzacarlton.com

Books by Demelza Carlton

Ocean's Gift series
Ocean's Gift (#1)
Ocean's Infiltrator (#2)
Ocean's Depths (#3)
Water and Fire

Turbulence and Triumph series
Ocean's Justice (#1)
Ocean's Trial (#2)
Ocean's Triumph (#3)
Ocean's Ride (#4)
Ocean's Cage (#5)
Ocean's Birth (#6)
How To Catch Crabs

Nightmares Trilogy
Nightmares of Caitlin Lockyer (#1)
Necessary Evil of Nathan Miller (#2)
Afterlife of Alana Miller (#3)

Mel Goes to Hell series
- Welcome to Hell (#1)
- See You in Hell (#2)
- Mel Goes to Hell (#3)
- To Hell and Back (#4)
- The Holiday From Hell (#5)
- All Hell Breaks Loose (#6)

Romance Island Resort series
- Maid for the Rock Star (#1)
- The Rock Star's Email Order Bride (#2)
- The Rock Star's Virginity (#3)
- The Rock Star and the Billionaire (#4)
- The Rock Star Wants A Wife (#5)
- The Rock Star's Wedding (#6)
- Maid for the South Pole (#7)
- Jailbird Bride (#8)

The Complex series
- Halcyon

Romance a Medieval Fairytale series
- Enchant: Beauty and the Beast Retold (#1)
- Awaken: Sleeping Beauty Retold (#2)
- Dance: Cinderella Retold (#3)
- Revel: Twelve Dancing Princesses Retold (#4)
- Silence: Little Mermaid Retold (#5)

Made in the USA
Lexington, KY
16 December 2019